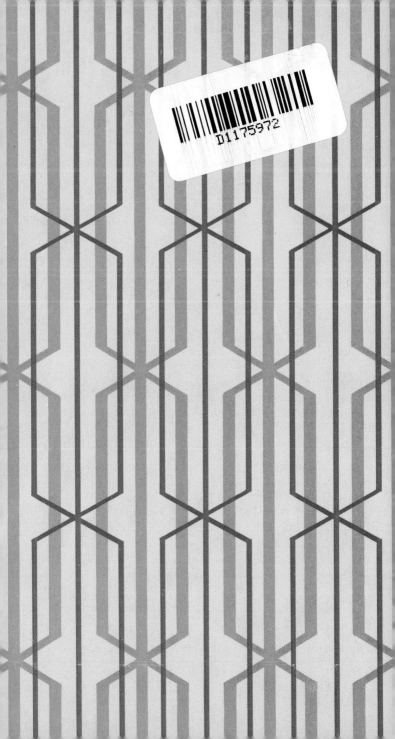

THE BAZAAR

THE BAZAAR
and other Stories

by

MARTIN DONISTHORPE ARMSTRONG

Short Story Index Reprint Series

BOOKS FOR LIBRARIES PRESS
FREEPORT, NEW YORK

First Published 1924
Reprinted 1970

STANDARD BOOK NUMBER:
8369-3278-1

LIBRARY OF CONGRESS CATALOG CARD NUMBER:
71-106242

PRINTED IN THE UNITED STATES OF AMERICA

Contents

Mrs. Barber's Christmas

OLD MRS. BARBER SAT ALONE IN HER wooden chair whose arms, gripped by the hands of three generations of grandmothers and grandfathers, were smoothed and worn till they looked like polished bones. The blinds were drawn, the lamp lighted, and a merry fire crackled in the grate where the kettle was juſt beginning to sing. At firſt its songs were far-off and sad —thin ghoſts of songs forgotten, but soon they settled to a warm homeliness like the comfortable purred song of a cat. And the two together— the sadness and the homeliness—soothed old Mrs. Barber till she really felt quite well again. That uncomfortable, dazed feeling in her head had gone and she settled down into a blurred, peaceful mood in which, like a spool unwinding itself, her mind effortlessly reproduced the doings of the day. Yes, on the whole she had enjoyed herself, and anyhow she was glad she had gone : Lizzy would have been hurt if she had not turned up for dinner on Chriſtmas Day. Four miles each way was a long walk but—well— she was glad she had gone, even though the walk back had almoſt been the death of her. Yes indeed, and if it hadn't been for Mr. Robson, the Lord knows what would have become of her. Directly she left Lizzy's to walk home again, she had felt it was going to be too much for her, and by the time she had done two miles she was feeling really bad. What a mercy that Mr. Robson in the cart had overtaken her and given her a lift for the rest of the way. And even then how ill she had felt : at one moment she really believed she was going to die in the cart, and when they stopped at her cottage Mr. Robson had to lift her down just as if she were a child again. Then she couldn't find her key, in fact she was feeling too ill to bother about it. All she wanted was to lie down, and if Mr. Robson had not held her up she actually would have lain down—just where she was, in the road. "Let me lie down. Let me lie down," she had whispered, and it was only after Mr. Robson had pretended to be angry with her that she had managed to pull herself together enough to remember where she had put the key. Then Mr. Robson had propped her against her door and forbidden her to lie down while he fastened his horse's reins to the railings, and after that he had unlocked her door and put her into her chair, and not only that but he had even made a fire for her and filled the kettle. Yes, he was a good fellow, was Robson, to bother so much about an old woman.

Once in her chair, she felt all right, she said, and so he had left her, promising to send his girl in an hour or two to see if she wanted anything.

And now she really did feel all right. The warmth of the fire seemed to be going right through her as though she were a pane of glass. It was grand. Mr. Robson certainly knew how to make a fire. . . . Yes, he was a good fellow, was Robson, to bother so much about an old woman. Sometimes a little shiver ran down her spine and the fire went blurred for a moment and seemed to recede from her, but that was rather nice, for it seemed to increase the sensation of tired well-being which had taken possession of her and rose sometimes on a little wave of ecstasy to a delicious feeling of numbness in her legs. As soon as the kettle boiled she would make herself a good strong cup of tea : and with a fire like that the kettle wouldn't be ·long . . . no . . . certainly Mr. Robson knew how to make a fire. . . . Yes . . . he was a good fellow, was Robson, to bother so much about ! . . .

The kettle suddenly began spluttering and she

roused herself to take it off the fire and fill the teapot.

"After all," said Mrs. Barber to Janie Robson, who had looked in when she was at her second cup, "after all, there's nothing like a good strong cup of tea for putting you right, no matter what's wrong. How anyone could get along without it, beats me. And yet there's the Bible. You won't find a word about tea from beginning to end. Wine, water, and milk, you'll find—'He asked for water and she gave him milk': that was Jael, you know; and then there's 'Wine to gladden man's heart,'—but seemingly they didn't go in for tea in those times. Well, there's no accounting for tastes." And then Mrs. Barber remembered again that it was Christmas Day and insisted on Janie running home. "You don't want to be bothered with an old woman on Christmas night, my dear," she said. "And tell your father from me that I'm doing nicely now."

At six o'clock the bells began to ring for the evening service: first one, clear and high in the darkness; then another, a deeper, warmer one; and soon all eight fell into their places in the scale. Over and over they tumbled down the length of the scale until there was no beginning and no ending to it, but just a continuous flow like water down a long waterfall. And then the bells suddenly changed places and wove in and out of one another on a new tune.

Mrs. Barber liked the bells. They produced in her a warm, mysterious, slightly ecstatic feeling, faintly recalling a long line of buried memories. "Dear me," she said to herself, shaking her head wonderingly. "Deary, deary me!" And suddenly she decided that she would go to church. Why not? It was just exactly what she was feeling inclined for. Besides, the distance was nothing, not a quarter of a mile. Well, if she was going she would have to get ready at once, and she got up—dear me, how stiff she was, to be sure!—and put on her bonnet and coat and a warm woollen muffler. Then she placed the matches on the edge of the table where she would be able to lay her hand on them in the dark, extinguished the lamp, and went out.

As she locked the door behind her, she felt as pleased and excited as a child on the brink of a secret escapade. It was a bitter night. She could feel the cold go right down her throat, and she pulled the muffler up over her mouth and nose. The road was like iron : her steps

13

knocked on it as though she were wearing clogs, and in the clear flinty darkness the grass in the ditches sparkled as if with a new-fallen shower of cryſtals. Her legs were ſtill a little weak, but then the diſtance was nothing, not a quarter of a mile, and she would have a long reſt in the church . . . an hour and ten minutes at leaſt . . . and coming back would be all down-hill . . . besides, the diſtance was nothing, not a l . . . The porch looked like a cold yellow cave at the end of the path between the tomb-ſtones, but when she passed through it and down the ſtep into the church, it was very far from being cold : it was deliciously warm, with a comfortable smell of hot-pipes and paraffin-oil. The crowd that flowed paſt her up the nave made her feel suddenly nervous and irritable and she took her seat far back among the empty pews where there would be no one to bother her or to notice if she did not ſtand up during the psalms.

From where she sat, the church looked like a huge softly-shining cavern upon whose floor the congregation was spread in a black, reſtless mass, out of which the pillars grew up, gradually more and more luminous, into the warm, miſty light like the ſtems of giant lilies. Lamps hung from

14

the arches and, far off in the distant chancel,
which appeared as a glowing core of radiance
beyond the paler light of the nave, the tall altar-
candles shone like a row of stars.

For Mrs. Barber's old eyes the many lamps
and candles filled the church with a golden fog,
and sometimes the lights receded from her, just
as it had happened at home when she was gazing
into the fire, or became suddenly blurred and
shed clusters of divergent rays downwards to
the floor and up into the darkness of the roof,
so that the whole cavern seemed full of blazing
comets. " Like the blessed stars of Heaven,"
Mrs. Barber murmured to herself, wondering
where the phrase had come from.

Then the organ began, building up out of
nothing just such a wonderful world for the ear
as the lights and pillars and arches had made
for the eyes : and soon there was a quiet stir
of white shapes in the chancel and she knew
that the choir had come in.

She listened delightedly to the intoning of
prayers and the rich, clear chanting of psalms
whose words were lost in the warm resonance of
the chancel, till the church seemed to brim up
with a shimmering lake of sound which washed
and soothed her tired brain. Then came the

hymn she had known all her life, and as she
stood, steadying herself by holding with both
hands on to the book-ledge, the lights and the
tall pillars and the black, uneven mass of the
congregation seemed to sway with the swaying
of the music. " O come, let us adore Him !
O come, let us adore Him ! " said the music,
climbing and climbing to the height from which
at last it curved so satisfyingly down to the
closing chord. The old words surged back into
her memory with the music—" God of God,
Light of Light . . . Very God, begotten not
created "—it had never occurred to her to wonder what they meant : their emotional meaning
for her was profound and sufficient and when
she sat down again she felt exhausted, more from
the intensity of her feelings than from the effort
of standing.

Far away in the chancel the monotone of an
unheard prayer rose again, but she did not
kneel. She felt that she must sit quite still for
a while, and then, as she raised her eyes, the
lights swam away from her again, hung aloft
and remote, and swung back large and blurred,
scattering long beams on the cowering congregation. " Like the blessed stars of Heaven,"
she whispered to herself again. Again the stars

16

swam upwards, up and up and up : it seemed, this time, as if they would never come back. They swam into a circle, then into another, circle above circle—like a crown—like a bride's cake, and Mrs. Barber could see now (so clearly that she wondered that she had failed to notice it before) that every star was a lighted taper held by an angel. There they stood, a calm, stationary whirlpool of angels, ascending whirl above whirl into infinite height.

Suddenly—so suddenly that Mrs. Barber jumped—they burst into song, a great chord of music, basses, tenors, altos, trebles, ringing and vibrating together till the sound of it drew her right out of herself and she saw herself receding upwards. Up and up and up she flew, till she was no more than a minute pin-point of light. Then her light expanded and she became herself again, as it were : and there she was, among the angels—a great crowd of them all facing one way. Their wings towered up before her and on each side of her : she could see every plume in minute detail, soft golden feathers laid perfectly one on another. She could not resist the impulse to put out her hand and stroke the wing in front of her. The angel looked round and his eyes smiled at her, but his mouth

17

did not stop singing. It seemed that they were all expecting some one—Mrs. Barber too felt the expectancy and suddenly their voices burst out again, but right in her ear this time, loud and startling. " Hallelujah ! Hallelujah ! " they sang, as though for the entrance of a king. And all at once they broke apart in front of her and curved away to the right and left, and she saw that some one was standing in the space which they had made. It was Jesus. He stood like a large, simple giant, twice as large as any of the angels, wrapped in a plain blue cloak. And then, as Mrs. Barber stood gazing at him, Jesus caught sight of her. She felt afraid just for a moment, but then he smiled as though he recognized her—such an extremely pleasant smile that at once she felt at ease. . . . It was nice of him to bother so much about. . . . But he was calling her. " Mrs. Barber ! " he was saying : and then, much louder, " Mrs. Barber ! " and again, alarmingly loud, " Mrs. Barber ! " " Yes, sir, yes ! " she said, trying in vain to move forward. And then a sudden giddiness came over her and everything was lost in a golden fog. " Come, Mrs. Barber," the voice went on. " Why, I declare : you've been asleep." " O no, sir," laughed Mrs. Barber, struggling to her feet. "Not asleep, sir!" But, all the same, she felt a little confused, a little dazed, because she was back in the church among "the blessed stars of Heaven,"—that is, among the lamps and candles—but now, somehow, the church was quite empty and she was going towards the door with the Vicar. How stiff and useless her legs were! It was so much more difficult to walk than to fly. She tried to explain to the Vicar : "It's difficult, you know, sir . . ." she said. "It's difficult after being up there." But though her legs were so helpless she was still glowing with happiness, and as they walked back to her cottage—apparently the Vicar was going to her cottage too— she told him, as well as she could, of the wonderful things she had seen. She wouldn't have told everybody, of course ; but the Vicar, being a clergyman, would understand. "And all the angels," she explained, "carried . . . carried . . . bells." Then she paused, perplexed. Surely that wasn't the word ? Bells ? No, how silly of her! It was tapers. "Yes, all the angels, sir, carried tapers. Wonderful ! You've no idea." But the Vicar was asking about her key, and he unlocked her door for her and lit the lamp and would not leave her until she had assured him that she was really quite well and had promised that she would go straight to bed. " O perfectly well, thank you, sir : and very, very happy."

She was too tired to undress : besides, she had promised the Vicar that she would get into bed at once. Yes, he was a good gentleman, was the Vicar . . . or was it Jesus ? or Mr. Robson ? . . . to bother so much about an old woman. . . . But all the angels were ringing bells . . . and the distance was nothing . . . not a quarter of a mile.

Helm Hall

THERE ARE EVENTS WHICH BE-
cause of their beauty, their terror, or some
strangeness, some poignancy about them, stand
alone in the memory, like secret islands, above
the general flow of experience with something
of the less-than-reality or more-than-reality of a
dream. It is as though one had paid a brief
visit to another life, another world—a visit
isolated by forgetfulness of the journeys thither
and thence. Such always remained for Richmond his visit to Helm Hall, an unpremeditated
visit thrust upon him by force of circumstances
and terminated at the first opportunity. The
force of circumstances was nothing more mysterious than the weather, though even the weather
that day *was*, in its sudden change, mysterious.
Richmond had walked far, seventeen miles or
more, across deserted moorlands rising into
gaunt hills of grey rock and dropping down
grey screes into bare valleys where spongy brown
bogs spotted with tussocks of coarse bent broke
out like sores amongst the heather.

The day was still and sunny, an autumn day
perfect for walking, and late in the afternoon
Richmond, leaving the grim moorland far above

him, had struck downwards into a hospitable
green country of meadows, richly wooded with
beech, oak and chestnut. There towards evening he sat down at the border of a wood to smoke
a pipe and consult his map. It took him some
time to locate his whereabouts. He had mis-
calculated, it turned out—had overshot by some
miles the road to the village for which he had
been aiming, and he was now, his map told
him, eight miles from the nearest hamlet—eight
miles, that is, from supper and a bed. Richmond realized, now that he had ceased walking,
that he was tired and very hungry, and he realized too with surprise that the sunlight had
suddenly gone out and that, though the evening
had been still when he sat down, now every leaf
was shivering and the great trees of the wood
were giving out a long fluctuating hiss like the
sea. He felt for the first time that day chilly,
and bent over his map again to decide at once
which direction to take. But even as he looked
at his map he was aware that the light was failing
rapidly, visibly before his eyes. The day was
drooping before its time—drooping almost to
twilight. The wind had stiffened and was
whirling and tossing the great boughs behind
him. He looked up at the sky : it was stormy

and swarmed with coiling strands of mist drifting layer above layer in vague and contrary
directions. Above the western horizon the eaves
of the storm hung over a cave of pale and angry
light, and looking down again he saw that he
was sitting in an emerald world. The trees,
the hedges, the fields, the silky moss on the
wall and railings, had become marvellously,
overwhelmingly green, not with the bright and
varied green of midday but with an intense
uniform emerald which, under the lightless sky,
seemed to be itself luminous. It was a world
in which light had changed places with dimness
in which the sky was dark as a forest floor and
the earth a thicket of luminous and swarming
vegetation. The wood behind him had changed
suddenly to a sinister cavern peopled with trunks
and twisted boughs, dark not with the darkness
of the shadows of day but with the darkness
of midnight. It was strange as an eclipse of
the sun. A sudden gust of heavy raindrops
pattered about him, leaving dark stains on his
clothes, and Richmond, having no waterproof,
retreated into the wood. At the far side of the
wood his map had shown an estate and a house
called Helm Hall. There, if the weather did not
improve, he would try to find a night's lodging.

There was no discoverable path through the wood, so he pushed as nearly as possible in a straight line, sometimes scrambling through thickets and screens of hanging boughs, sometimes walking upright among tall trunks as if exploring a dark and draughty church.

He had judged fairly well, for when he emerged he could see under a cold silvery light the peaks of high roofs among black elm trees. The rain had not yet begun in earnest, but it came in splashes on the wind-gusts and as he left the wood the boughs streamed out after him on the draught.

It was an old, a very old house. Gaunt but beautiful in the twilight it stood, a noble terminus to its grass-grown drive. The windows, lightless and uncurtained, glared blindly at the gathering storm. Some were open and, high up, one, unfastened, slammed itself shut from time to time, startling the stillness. Richmond approached with misgiving : the place was so evidently deserted. But at least it was worth while to go round to the back : there surely he would find servants, or at least a caretaker.

He tiptoed down the gravel path which skirted the house, and when he reached the back entrance he was surprised and relieved to find the door half open. No lights were visible and he knocked, it seemed, to an empty house, so hollowly did his knocking resound, so intrusively on what felt like a silence of years. And no one came to the door though he knocked and waited three times ; no one came and no sound inside the house responded to his knocking. He pushed open the door and went in. It was colder in there than out-of-doors and the place smelt damp and earthy. On the right and left were kitchens and larders, empty and unmistakably disused. Richmond began on the tips of his toes to penetrate deeper into the house. It was thrilling and a little creepy, this exploration of a dark, unknown, and noiseless house, and the nervous anticipation of a sudden meeting. There was a closed door at the end of the passage : he cautiously opened it and found himself in a high and draughty hall. A grey light fell from mullioned windows on to a wide staircase—a light so sparse and watery that he seemed to be standing in a great cave full of the sea. Dark shapes of tables, chairs and screens showed like dim rocks and reefs ; dim banners hung like seaweed from above ; the draughty air touched his face and hands like the cold, invisible undulations of water, and with the soft buffeting of waves the gusty wind beat against the windows.

Still more thrilled, still more wonderingly alarmed, he crossed to the staircase and began to go up. Thick carpet muffled his tread as he ascended higher and higher in the hollow of the great cavern.

He turned off, at the top, into a narrow channel with the faint, rare print of windows on its darkened walls. At the end, the passage turned to the left, he found, but just as he was about to follow it a strange thing happened, for a light shone out of the wall close beside him, making him start and instantly face to his right, and immediately afterwards a voice behind him made him spin round again the other way, to find another light held, it seemed, by some one far down the passage. Richmond stood immovable : that was his first instinct. The next was to face again the first light which was so startlingly close to him. When he did so he realized that he was gazing into the dim pool of a mirror and that this light was merely the reflection of the other. The voice called again—a tremulous, asthmatic, old-man's voice—" Mary ? Is that you, Mary ? " and he saw now behind the light an old face staring blindly down the passage.

26

" I see you," the voice went on. " It's no good your prowling about like that, worrying the life out of me. Go away, I tell you, and leave me in peace."

Richmond began to walk down the passage towards the light. " It's all right," he said. " It's me ! "

" Who are you ? " quavered the voice, and as Richmond came within the range of the light, the old man stared at him with frightened, inquiring eyes.

" Did you see her ? " he asked in a whisper, " as you came up the stairs ? "

" I saw no one," said Richmond, and he began trying to explain his presence there. But the old man stared at him stupidly, apprehensively, paying no attention, obviously, to what Richmond was saying.

" I know what you've come for," he said suspiciously. " You've come after *her*. I knew they'd send, sooner or later. Well, you can look. You'll not find her : she's gone."

" I'm looking for no one," said Richmond, " and nothing, but somewhere to spend the night, and perhaps something to eat, if you have anything to spare."

The old man beckoned him into the room

from which he had emerged. It was a comfortable modern room ; there were arm-chairs and cupboards, a red and white checked cloth covered the table, there was a cheerful commonplace paper on the walls and a large iron bedstead filled one of the corners. A fire crackled in the grate where a kettle was sending out a plume of steam which curled back and was drawn up the chimney. The room, Richmond told himself, had probably been the housekeeper's room.

Still suspicious and irresolute the old man stood looking at him until Richmond repeated his request for food, at which he went to a cupboard and brought out bread, a pot of jam, a teapot and tea-things. He began to make tea and when it was made he stood again silently watching Richmond eat and drink.

" How did you get in ? " he asked suddenly.

" By the back door," said Richmond. " I found it open. It's open still : so are the windows, and one of them's unfastened. You'll be having broken glass with this storm."

" I must close in," said the old man as though making a desperate resolution, and he took up the lamp and was on the point of leaving Richmond in the dark.

" Hold on, there ! What are you doing ? "

28

shouted Richmond, surprised into sudden asperity.
" Can't you get another light ? "

The old man seemed for a moment puzzled.
Then he went to the cupboard and got out a
candle and again, with the candle in his hand,
he stood watching Richmond. " If I wait till
you're finished," he asked with a wheedling
smile, " will you come with me ? "

" Yes, I'll come," said Richmond, glad not
to let the unaccountable old creature out of his
sight ; and a quarter of an hour later, candle
in hand, they went out into the passage and
again the reflected light swam obediently into
sight in the mirror at the end of the passage.
For the moment Richmond had forgotten all
about the mirror : at the appearance of the
light he started and the old man, too, suddenly
stood still.

" You saw her ? " he whispered sharply,
pointing down the passage. " Down there
with the light. That was her on her prowls
again."

" That," answered Richmond, once more self-
possessed, " was our reflection in the mirror."

" You may think so," said the old man,
searching Richmond's face with horrible dis-
traught eyes. Then he pushed his face close

up to Richmond's and added with intense significance, " *I* know better."

A turn in the passage hid the mirror and they began a long progress down dark corridors and into tall gaunt bedrooms with towering four-poster beds, under whose doors, as they pushed them open, the draught whistled and shrivelled their candle to a fluttering blue spark. So they went, spasmodically disturbing the windy silence by the solemn shutting of windows and doors.

After many of such rooms they entered one larger than the rest. A tall bed canopied with black and gold taffeta rose before them near the door and in the middle of the room stood a large, heavily carved writing table set with tall candlesticks and with a high-backed chair drawn up to it. " This was her room," said the old man, standing as if fascinated over the writing-table. " And this is where they found her."

" Found whom ? " asked Richmond.

" Who ? Why, Miss Lucy, of course, poor thing."

" Indeed," said Richmond, who had ceased to look for much meaning in the old man's ramblings. " And what was she doing ? "

"Doing?" said the old fellow, turning on Richmond with amazement. "Doing? She was dead. Yes, sitting in that chair with her arms on the desk and her head laid on her arms, dead. She'd taken poison, poor thing."

The wind beat and fluttered at the window like a great struggling bird and through the black horizontal boughs of a cedar a sudden cold blaze of moonlight, escaped from a rent in the flying clouds, filled the room with a wild chequer of black and white, illuminating fragments of bed, walls and furniture, calling a hint of dark red from the carpet, raising to a fantastic tallness the black candlesticks on the writing table, and printing a scar like leprosy on the left side of the old man's face.

It had come and gone in three seconds, a grim and ghostly revelation. But to the old man it meant nothing : he stood there immovable, fascinated by the writing-table, until Richmond led him away.

They ascended a stair to the next floor. Above them the thud of an unfastened window reverberated dully in the hollow upper story.

"You heard that?" whispered the old man, stopping short on the stairs and facing Richmond. "That's her again on her prowls. She often goes round like this when I'm closing in. Sometimes she's ahead and sometimes she's behind ! "

" But why ? " objected Richmond, with some idea of arguing him out of his fancies.

" Why ? Because she's trying to get back, don't you see."

" Whom are you speaking of ? Miss Lucy ? " asked Richmond bluntly.

" Miss Lucy ? No, *she* wanted to die, poor thing. There ! " he whispered, as the drum-beat of the window resounded again. " There she goes. I'd rather she came back than kept prowling round out of sight like that."

" That was the unfastened window I told you about," said Richmond.

" Ah, I wish it was. I wish it was," muttered the old fellow with the same knowing gleam in his eye.

On the top story the rain was blowing in through the open dormers, timbers creaked in the roof above, and periodic gusts smote the slating like a bursting wave, shaking, it seemed, the whole great house.

A steep back-stair took them down to the ground floor. A door at the bottom was shut and the old man paused before opening it.

" Wait ! " he whispered. " She may be there ! "
and with infinite caution he turned the handle
and peered apprehensively round the door.
" I've sometimes heard her in the kitchen," he
explained, holding the candle high as he shut
the door behind them.

The smell of dampness and earth took Richmond back to his first stealthy arrival, so recent
and yet (looked back upon through the dim
phantasmagoric world into which he had stepped
from the world outside) so remote already, so
buried beneath vivid and disquieting unrealities.
Yes, that short day's-end seemed like the experience of a week with its impressions of vague
darkness, moving candlelight, the broken sounds
of storm about the house and the sense of tragedy
within. Upon Richmond, a prey to weariness
and this strange isolation from saneness and
reality, all these things were beginning to exercise a disquieting influence, and the restless and
shadowy presence of Mary was becoming for
him something more than the disordered fancies
of this horrible old man.

Rain and a chill draught blew in at the back
door. The old man shut and bolted it and
they made their way down the stone-flagged
passage and into the great hall. The wind still

beat at the windows but now the great cold place was almost pitch-dark and the candle which the old man set down on the table showed only pale and misty surfaces beyond the golden haze which englobed it.

" This," began the old man—he seemed now to think that he was showing sightseers over the house and his voice had the flat, inhuman quality of a man's who talks in his sleep—" This is the great hall, formerly the banqueting hall, a portion of the original Priory built in thirteen twenty-one for the Lady Anne Valery." Loud and startling, a volley of raindrops beat like the clatter of finger-nails against the window-panes, but more startling still was the old man's shriek. " It's her. It's her," he screamed, and, rushing to a casement in the great window, he flung it open. A gust of rain burst into the hall : the flying drops drummed like hail on the wooden floor.

" Mary ! Mary ! " he shouted in his thin, asthmatic voice, leaning out into the rain. " Come here : come in, my dear. For God's sake, come in out of the rain." Then his hands slipped from the window-ledge and he fell forward, the upper half of his body hanging limply over the sill. Richmond dragged him in and shut the window. His face was white and glazed with rain : in his staring eyes the pupils dilated and contracted spasmodically. Even after Richmond had got him upstairs into the housekeeper's room and established him in a chair before the fire he remained inert and stupefied, paying no attention to anything Richmond said or did.

Richmond in the end determined to make his own arrangements for the night. He searched drawers and cupboards and at last found some blankets and a packet of candles. These he carried into the nearest bedroom and made up a bed for himself on a sofa at the foot of the great four-poster. When he returned after making these preparations he found the old man smoking a pipe. He seemed to have grown accustomed to Richmond and turning round in his chair he asked him—" Well, and what do you think of the house ? "

The sudden change to the commonplace of sanity was startling. " The house ? " Richmond replied. " Oh, I think it's extraordinary ! "

The old man's expression changed. " Ah," he whispered : " *do* you now ? You notice something *extraordinary* about it ? "

A feeling of weariness and disgust came over

Richmond and he cut the old man short. " I'm going to bed," he said.

He locked himself into his bedroom and, setting down his candle upon a table, he lit two other candles from it and set them in tall candlesticks on the mantelpiece. As their light grew, the dim vacancy of a mirror loomed up behind them, so that they seemed to stand on a threshold between two grey and hollow caverns, the one hardly more real than the other. Richmond took off some of his clothes, and made himself as comfortable as possible on the sofa. The wind rumbled heavily in the wide chimney ; wind and rain beat upon the window, through which he could see a dark confusion of whirling boughs, and it seemed to Richmond as he lay there that he was lying in the stateroom of a great, rolling galleon. . . .

Next morning he awoke early. In the bright reality of the sunshine which streamed in at the tall window the memory of last night seemed a remote nightmare : he felt as if he had awoken from the delirious fancies of fever into perfect health. Looking about him he noticed for the first time the beauty and richness of his room. Then the sight of the two half-burnt candles which he had placed last night on the mantelpiece suddenly brought the reality of yesterday vividly before him. The thought of the old man filled him with loathing and he rose from his sofa and began to dress, determined to leave the place as quickly as possible. Above all, he felt, he must get away without seeing the old creature again, and leaving some money on the table he took up his knapsack and went out.

As he passed the old man's door he noticed that it was open. He ran noiselessly downstairs, crossed the hall, and was hurrying down the back passage when he heard footsteps on the gravel outside approaching the back door. A sensation of disgust overcame him. For Richmond now the old man was a part of a sinister yesterday, a symbol of fever and madness, and the thought of seeing him rise again out of the past was horrible to him. A half-open door was beside him. He stepped quickly through it to wait unseen until the old man had passed, and found himself in a damp, ill-smelling store-room. Long streaks of mould scarred the plaster of the walls and a large wet stain darkened the stone floor. Richmond found himself staring at the stain and with a feeling of sickness he suddenly became convinced that it was a half-dried pool of blood. The footsteps were coming down the passage. They were on the point of passing his door. Suddenly they paused and, raising his eyes, Richmond saw the old man's face looking at him round the door. "A—h !" he said, in his horrible asthmatic voice. "I thought so. So *that's* what you were after all the time."

The face vanished and Richmond heard him hurrying down the passage again towards the back door, and as he darted out after him into the passage he saw him disappear into the kitchen, slamming the back door shut as he passed it.

But when Richmond reached the door the old man was back again, ready for him. His eyes gleamed insanely and he stood with his hands close to his sides, turning where he stood, oddly, mechanically, like a marionette or a weathercock, so as to keep Richmond always in front of him. Then Richmond noticed something hanging from his right hand. It was a chopper. Neither spoke. Richmond steadily returned the old man's stare, and so they stood —it seemed as if they would always stand thus —tensely and silently watching one another. Suddenly Richmond spoke, loudly and decisively.

"Put that chopper down," he said. The old

38

man at firſt did nothing : then his ſtare wavered
and the chopper dropped from his hand.

"Now open the door," Richmond ordered.
The old man obeyed.

Once out of doors, Richmond ran. Round
to the front of the house he ran and down the
long, grass-grown drive, and when at laſt he
ſtopped and looked back it was not too late for
a laſt glimpse of the old, many-windowed house,
silent and venerable among its dark elm-boughs,
above which a circling flight of pigeons shone
suddenly silver in the clear autumn sunlight.

Symphony in G Minor

IN A RABBIT POACHED, SO A CON-firmed poacher once confided to me, one takes a pride and a joy which are not to be obtained from a dozen rabbits gained in lawful sport. It is the same, I find, with conversation. I am far from being averse to conversation, but how much more intriguing, as a rule, are the conversations on one's right or left. For me, garden-parties and At-Homes are endurable only because they provide opportunities for eavesdropping upon the conversation of others. It is true that when one is at the same time oneself engaged in conversation this practice is perilous, for one may soon find oneself insulting one's partner, or offering, in place of ardent affirmatives, absent-minded nega-tives which may permanently ruin one's repu-tation.

But the risk is worth the entertainment, as I realized once more when I sat yesterday in the Jeffersons' garden conversing ostensibly with Mrs. Murgatroyd but in truth " listening-in " surreptitiously to a conversation on my left between Ledbitter the musical critic and some one else whose voice I did not know. Ledbitter is an admirable talker, and I edged unostentatiously to my left.

" O, I agree with you in theory," he was saying, " in your objection to programme music. Unrepresentational music is, theoretically, the only pure form of music. But in practice is any music, in the end, unrepresentational? It may represent one thing to the composer and other things to each listener, but, I often suspect, it always represents *something* to everybody. Let me give you an example. I went last week to Southwark Cathedral and there I heard an orchestral performance of a Mozart Symphony. The incongruity of the thing and an uncomfortable seat must have blunted my æsthetic sense and aroused instead a gang of literary demons who proceeded to act the following pantomime."

I switched over to Mrs. Murgatroyd. She was safely embarked on a speech about servants which would surely need little punctuation from me. I switched back to Ledbitter.

" Two lackeys carrying tapers," he was saying, "entered the dark saloon and in the depths of the gilded mirrors twenty tapers glided and twinkled in reply, and great patches of red brocade and red carpet glowed or faded as the taper-bearers moved from place to place. A thick, warm smell of felt, velvet and woodwork pervaded the air.

"Each at opposite sides of the saloon, the lackeys proceeded to light the candles in the gold and crystal candelabra between the rococo mirrors, till the darkness was chased by degrees to the top end of the room and then out of the room altogether, and the saloon, from wall to wall, was brimmed with yellow candlelight. Thus illuminated, it appeared like the inside of a great box, impervious to daylight and fresh air, lined throughout with heavy red stuffs—velvet, brocade and felt—except for the gold and white doors in the side walls and the great folding doors at the end, flanked by the marble figures of nude, well-nourished ladies—goddesses whom a little brocade might have changed into grand-duchesses.

"Now, on the dais at the top end of the saloon, the lackeys were arranging chairs and music-stands for the orchestra, and, that done, they began to prepare the auditorium, drawing forward from the wall the two grand-ducal arm-chairs. They, too, were gilt and upholstered in red velvet, and on the padded backs and the cushions of the seats were embroidered the grand-ducal arms and crown. On either side

of them and behind, row after row, uncomfortable chairs were set for the *entourage* and a few
favoured guests. A table was placed in front
of their Highnesses' chairs and the great folding
doors were thrown open. The saloon was ready.

"From one of the side doors the orchestra
filed on to the dais ; with a rattling of chairs
and music-stands they took their places, and the
subtle and beautiful discord of tuning arose.
Then followed an expectant silence, during which
the musicians assumed abstracted expressions.
Some threw back their heads and drew long
breaths. A nervous clarinet, still uncertain of
itself, broke in upon the stillness with its timid
and plaintive bleat, at which the plump first
fiddle turned himself in the direction of the
sound as though annoyed by the cry of some
strange animal. Little Herr Mozart, the new
Kapellmeister, was seen to be standing at one
of the doors. There was a rustle of silk, the
muffled sound of shoes on a felt drugget, and
the Grand Duke and Duchess of Hohenstaufen-
Lindeberg entered through the folding doors,
and, followed by the company, advanced up the
aisle between the rows of gilded chairs. With
tilted noses and looking curiously about them,
they advanced at a leisurely pace like a pair of

43

geese, so leisurely that the company in the rear were jostling those in front who had been forced to check their pace in conformity with that of their Highnesses.

"The Grand Duke of Hohenstaufen-Lindeberg was clean-shaven. A pronounced and well-shaped nose and chin protruded from a huge, grey wig ; a portly stomach swelled before and portly calves behind ; the right hand, holding a lorgnon, displayed a well-turned wrist. His Grand Duchess, too, was massive. Most noticeable in her large, red face were the great, finely-chiselled nose and the high, receding forehead, above which the powdered wig and head-dress rose tier upon tier. As she advanced, her coiffure sailed up the saloon like a full-rigged ship.

"The orchestra sprang to its feet. At the foot of the dais in front of it Herr Mozart was bowing. His Highness acknowledged with a slight gesture of the lorgnon ; Her Highness made no acknowledgment at all. They took their seats. The Grand Duchess, placing her fan and vinaigrette on the table before her, pursed her lips and threw back her head. The hawklike nose, the lofty forehead, wig, and head-dress superimposed one upon another, composed a formidable profile. The Grand Duke beckoned to Herr Mozart. Herr Mozart approached, blushing with pleasure. He appeared little more than a boy : short, slim, with clear-cut delicate features and pink complexion, he looked in his neat wig, lace frill, and buckled shoes, like an exquisite little bit of Dresden.

'And your Symphony, *Kapellmeister !*' asked His Highness. 'We are to hear it to-night ?'

'If Your Highness pleases,' replied Herr Mozart. 'It is finished and we have practised it several times.'

'Then let us hear it by all means. But first let us have the new *Suite* by His Highness my brother-in-law. You have practised it ?'

'Yes, Your Highness, and I put it down for this evening in accordance with Your Highness's instructions.'

'Good. Pray begin at once, then, *Kapell-meister*. The company, I see, is seated.' Herr Mozart ascended the dais, tapped with his *bâton* on the desk, and His Highness's brother-in-law's new *Suite* began.

"It was a highly enjoyable piece of music, correct in every particular. The *Sarabande* was easily distinguished from the *Gigue*, and the *Minuet* had four crochets in a bar. There was nothing, literally nothing, that one would wish to alter.

45

"Next came Herr Mozart's *Symphony*. Some of the candles were guttering and their wax dripped on to the floor ; the lackeys went round attending to them. In the mirrors the massed heads of the company were reflected in steep gradient, topped by the mirrors and hangings of the opposite wall ; their cold depths seemed not only to reflect but also slightly to criticize the august assembly. Herr Mozart's Symphony also reflected the august assembly, and not only the assembly but all the little formal society that clustered round the grand-ducal court. But where the mirrors had criticized, the Symphony idealized. Like a lens, it gathered the period into an exquisite miniature in which all the crudities and grossnesses of reality were refined into delicate art, and Lindeberg and its society appeared in the guise of a delicious Arcadia. In a word, the Symphony was the work of supreme genius ; already, before the end of the first movement, the Grand Duke and Duchess had nodded and whispered that the new *Kapellmeister* was quite satisfactory. But the august assembly did not perceive how the music pictured them, how it was they themselves who were represented in the beautiful young shepherds and shepherdesses, satin-clad

46

and aristocratic, who led real lambs on leashes of pink and blue ribbon ; nor how the gilded convolutions of the rococo mirrors broke, in the music, into fresh, green leafage ; how the candle-flames changed into real stars, not scattered untidily over the heavens, but arranged in pretty patterns, while in little geometrical bowers lovers conversed in words of an exquisite tenderness. Nor were they aware that the music would preserve for future generations not only the charm of their little society, but also its ludicrous limitations. But, though they did not perceive these things, like all listeners they identified themselves with the moods of the music. The Grand Duchess sighed softly, for, while she unconsciously nodded her full-rigged head to the music and tapped her fan against her ample thigh, she felt herself young and beautiful, dancing among charming young men who re-sembled Herr Mozart and executing sudden little provocative sallies, sudden demure retreats.

" The Grand Duke fancied that in a comfort-able bower of roses he was pressing the hand and whispering passionate words into the ear of Frau von Etlingen, the plump Lady-in-Waiting to his Consort. The gentlemen of the company crossed their legs and shook regretful heads over lost opportunities ; the ladies sighed under a gentle oppression not wholly due to the tightness of their stays.

"At the end of the *Adagio* a secretary came and whispered in the ear of the Grand Duke, who rose and went out. Matters of high importance (relative to the painting and upholstering of the new barouche) claimed his attention, and he was detained, discussing and signing documents, for three-quarters of an hour.

"When the Symphony was finished the Grand Duchess summoned the *Kapellmeister*. As he approached her, she was assailed by the curious desire to take him on her knee and give him a kiss and a chocolate, but, instead, she made him sit for a moment in the Grand Duke's vacant chair.

'Your Symphony is charming, *Kapellmeister*,' she said. 'His Highness and I especially liked the second movement—the *Allegro Vivace*, was it not ? '

'Your Highness refers to the *Adagio* ? ' said Herr Mozart in a voice which trembled with gratitude and emotion.

'To be sure ! The *Adagio* ! So elegant, so melodious ! We wish to hear the Symphony again.' Tears stood in Herr Mozart's eyes.

It seemed to him that he had achieved the crown of his ambitions.

' Next Wednesday ? ' Her Highness went on. ' *Ach, nein !* Not next Wednesday, for on that day Prince Heinrich will be here and the Grand Duke himself is composing an Overture for the occasion. But Saturday will do. Let it be Saturday, please, *Kapellmeister*. And now, what are you going to play ? '

' A *Minuet* by Lully, if Your Highness permits.'

' Good. I love French music above all other.' Herr Mozart bent over Her Highness's hand in an ecstasy of simple devotion.

"The Grand Duke returned in time for the Minuet and at the end of the concert he again called his *Kapellmeister* to him. ' *Kapellmeister*,' he said, ' I am myself composing an Overture for the occasion of Prince Heinrich's visit. But I am not altogether satisfied with my main theme : I am having difficulty, too, with the brass, and indeed with the strings and the wood-wind, and little time remains. Now I am much pleased with your Symphony : your style is excellent, so that I feel sure that you are competent to set matters right for me. Pray come to-morrow morning at ten o'clock.'

"Herr Mozart bowed and departed, flushed with pride and pleasure at the thought that His Highness had called him in to assist in so important a matter, for which he willingly abandoned the new string quartet upon which he was then engaged.

"Such," concluded Ledbitter, "was the pantomime which those deceiving demons displayed to me. In no particular do the incidents in it appear to tally with biographical and historical fact. Mozart was no longer a youth when he wrote the symphony in question : Lindeberg is not to be found upon the map : the Grand Duke and Duchess of Hohenstaufen-Lindeberg are, it seems, pure imposture and, so far as I can ascertain, they never kept a barouche."

Laughter from his unknown partner greeted the end of Ledbitter's anecdote, and so absorbed had I too been in it that I laughed also and awoke to the fact that I was laughing in the face of Mrs. Murgatroyd, whose expression, as she met my gaze, was the reverse of mirthful.

"And you honestly mean to tell me," she said, "that you would like to see Bolshevism established in England ? "

The Bazaar

"I TELL YOU," SAID MR. CATCHPOLE to his sister, "that if you wish to raise the money you will have to háve a bazaar."

"Dear James," answered Miss Catchpole, "for a philosopher you are very unreasonable. Consider the absurdity of a bazaar. One writes to all one's friends begging for material : one invites them to become stallholders : after weeks spent in accumulating a number of things which no one wants, one hires a hall at great expense : one persuades the nearest Countess to open the bazaar, and then every one grumbles at the necessity of having to come and buy. In the end, it is true, you get your money, but by how unreasonable, how extravagant a method. Now my method is simple and economical. From the people from whom you would beg material for the bazaar I simply beg the money direct. As I have said, considering that you are a philosopher, your suggestion is most unreasonable."

"But, dear Elenor," said Mr. Catchpole, "it is precisely because I am a philosopher that my suggestion is unreasonable. I realize—and you, for all your good sense, do not—that human beings never take the reasonable course.

So rational a method as you suggest would horrify them and, worse still, it would produce not money but excuses. No, Elenor, the days of miracles are past. Nowadays one must be content to set in motion a process and I suggested a bazaar because the bazaar is a profoundly interesting physiological, perhaps even a pathological, phenomenon. You promote as it were a ferment among your victims which eventually produces the money by natural means. You cannot fly in the face of Nature, and unhappily Nature is always wasteful. Remember the Geranio-Pelargonian War, or, for that matter, any other war."

"But I know nothing of the Geranio-Pelargonian War."

"Then allow me to tell you about it." Mr. Catchpole wriggled himself farther back into his arm-chair and began as follows :

"The kings of Gerania and Pelargonia sat together on the terrace of the palace overlooking the plain which divided their realms. They had dined well and now they lingered over their third bottle of Château Toxique, that peerless wine grown in the royal vineyards that lay at their feet. Being kings, they did not descend to the topics of ordinary men, and even now in that after-dinner leisure their talk was of international affairs, for they were comparing with some heat the ladies of Pelargonia with those of Gerania. At length, when the king of Gerania, in the attempt to elucidate a point, had mentioned that the ladies of Pelargonia were notoriously inferior in the matter of ankles, the king of Pelargonia felt compelled to emphasize the opposite view by punching the nose of his guest.

"Such a conflict of national interests could not long remain limited to individuals, and soon all Gerania (so the Geranian newspapers declared) was thrilled to its foundations, and the great heart of the Pelargonian public (the Pelargonian Press registered it unanimously) beat with a profound and generous indignation. The public of each nation read the papers and was surprised to learn that these strong emotions were surging in its midst : each individual reproached himself with callousness and made up for it by working himself up into a state of great excitement. A week later, war was declared amid scenes of unparalleled enthusiasm in both countries. The Geranians averred that they would fight till the possibility of such aggression was eternally abolished : Pelargonia solemnly stated that nothing but her abiding love of peace had driven her to declare war.

" The two armies advanced against one another across the rich plains which divided the two kingdoms and, halting in time to allow the regulation space between their opposing lines, dug themselves in, brought up their artillery, and set about shelling No-Man's-Land in accordance with military procedure. The customary routine of warfare had begun.

" Over the details of the war it is unnecessary to linger. Both nations alternately achieved gratifying successes and suffered disquieting reverses, and their respective Press-bureaux magnified the successes into the most brilliant victories known to history and proved that the reverses were evidence of acute strategy on the part of their generals. Both Geranians and Pelargonians advanced and retreated across the same tract of country half-a-dozen times with no other result than to spread ruin across a land already ruined and to slaughter or mutilate thousands of the flower of their manhood.

" Meanwhile the non-combatant part of the Pelargonian people sat at home and read *The Pelargonian Mercury*. ' In consequence,' they read, ' of a series of brilliant operations carried out during the last week, our troops have occupied a new position on a two-mile front. The new line is one of great strength. The surprise of the enemy was complete and their casualties extremely heavy.'

"News of this description invariably called forth the greatest jubilation : a general holiday was declared and the church-bells rang continuously for twenty-four hours. But so depressing was the effect of the casualty-lists subsequently published that only another brilliant victory availed to restore the broken spirits of the nation.

"*The Geranian Times* produced equally stimulating fare for non-combatant Gerania in statements such as this : ' Early this morning after two days' artillery preparation our troops attacked on a wide front and were soon in possession of the enemy's front and support lines. It has been impossible to estimate the enemy's casualties, which amounted to many thousands.'

"On such occasions all Gerania thrilled with enthusiasm : effigies of the king of Pelargonia were burnt in every public square and a salvo of a hundred guns fired from the citadel broke every window in the metropolis.

"So the war continued, week in, week out,

until at the end of a year Gerania found her army decimated and her treasury empty. Thereupon, in the name of civilization and humanity, she offered humiliating terms to the enemy. These the Pelargonians indignantly refused and the war continued. · Soon, however, the unbroken silence from both directions proved that on neither side was there anyone left to kill. The long struggle was over.

" National feeling, thus deprived of its proper outlet, at once broke out both in Gerania and Pelargonia into revolutions which drove their kings into exile and set up republics in their place. Thereupon each country declared with perfect truth that the enemy was beaten, and terms, so carefully worded that to each side they seemed honourable to itself and humiliating to the enemy, were drawn up and signed. Both nations maintained that the objects for which they had fought had been fully accomplished ; and this, as it happens, was true, for though bread, which before the war had cost a penny a loaf, was now at a shilling, and wine, previously fourpence, was now four shillings a pint, yet the Château Toxique vineyards had been totally obliterated and the price of that famous wine had risen even beyond the reach of kings. Besides, the kings themselves were no longer there to buy it.

"Now you, my dear Elenor," concluded Mr. Catchpole, "with your economical and reasonable mind will no doubt denounce all this as extravagant lunacy. To slaughter the better half of the manhood of two nations, to cripple both for half a century, and to lay waste fifty square miles of the fairest and most fruitful lands in Europe is, ·I admit, a clumsy method of removing a couple of undesirable persons and a few square yards of too stimulating vineyard. But Nature, Elenor, is neither reasonable nor economical and, if you insist on assuming that she is, I fear that you will collect no money whatever for your deserving charity."

The Birthday

SHE SAT, POOR SENTIMENTAL MRS. Hetherington, at her piano playing the simple and more plaintive passages of Chopin's Nocturnes. Chopin soothed Mrs. Hetherington, though it is certain that, if Chopin could have heard her interpretation of him, Mrs. Hetherington would not have soothed Chopin, for she took amazing liberties with him, drove him into sudden little gushing sallies and hung him up on wistful pauses incredibly protracted, forcing him, poor Chopin, to express all the vague impossible longings of her sentimental, self-afflicted soul. It was half-past ten in the morning. Mr. Hetherington and Louis had long since departed for the office and Mrs. Hetherington herself had already given out the stores and had been to the kitchen to order to-night's dinner and to-morrow's breakfast. As for lunch, well, as she was accustomed to say, with a martyred smile, " a poached egg is always enough for me." Now she had the whole day in front of her till six o'clock, when her men returned : the whole day and nothing to do, and to-day of all days ! She had foreseen it last night : they would forget again this year, and sure enough this morning at breakfast not a sign from either of them. She had gazed at them both with large, reproachful eyes ; they had noticed it, both of them. "Had a bad night, Mother ? " · her husband had asked, and she had shaken her head sadly. "A head-ache ? " Louis had suggested. "No, not a headache to-day."

And they had left it at that, for they had been accustomed for years to these melancholy mysteries. She demanded so much, did Mrs. Hetherington, a constant homage of embraces, a continuous supply of spoken sympathy which it was beyond human power to provide. Nothing for her was certain that was not continually being expressed. As for herself, she was always expressing. She had pet names for both of them. Her husband was Faidie, a name extraordinarily unsuited to him, and her way of using it had an obviously chilling effect on him which she strove to overcome by using it more frequently. And it was the same with Loo-Loo : her ceaseless endearments bothered and oppressed him and her ridiculous nickname covered the poor boy with shame. She was always caressing him, asking him if he felt unwell and if he was warm enough, or offering her cheek for a kiss at the most inopportune moments. And she would embarrass them both by recalling intimate reminiscences of the past in the presence of strangers. "Do you remember, Faidie dear," she would say, casting down her eyes, "that lovely afternoon at Pangbourne soon after our engagement, when you made that remark about my voice ? . . ."

"Voice ? " replied Mr. Hetherington. "A little sore throat, was it, Mother ? " and she would abandon the reminiscence with a gesture of despair.

"Your Mother unfortunately has no sense of decency," Mr. Hetherington would remark afterwards to Louis.

Such was their home life. She demanded so much, exorbitant Mrs. Hetherington, that there was nothing left for them to give : indeed they checked their giving in the hope of checking her endless and embarrassing demands. She drove them continually to take refuge from her.

And Mrs. Hetherington accounted for it by saying that neither her Faidie nor her Loo-Loo ever *really* understood her.

Yet on occasions when she forgot these grievances she discovered, on looking back afterwards, that she had quite enjoyed herself.

For a whole evening, sometimes, she and Faidie
and Louis would talk and laugh with great
good-humour ; and then there were those
delightful evenings when they had a few friends
to dinner and Faidie complimented her on the
arrangement of the table and the excellence of
the menu, and Louis stared at her in amazement
when she came down dressed for the occasion,
exclaiming, " I say, Mater, you *are* a swell ! "
and after dinner, in the drawing-room, Louis
would tell ridiculous stories about her, of how
once when Father sent her a wire from town
she had declared that it couldn't be from him
because it wasn't in his writing ; or how she
would not allow the waiting-maid to put his
letters on his breakfast-plate for fear the post-
man's children had chicken-pox. " He makes
such fun of me, you know ! " she would say,
casting up her eyes and laughing with the rest.
Yes, charming evenings !

And yet, when she reflected on it, even her
friends did not really understand her. That
was the worst of having such an unusual nature :
so few people could sympathize. No, her friends
valued her simply because of Faidie and Louis.
" If I were alone," she said, " they would never
come near me," and she sighed patiently.

It was so hard simply to be made a convenience of : and, when you came to think of it, so dishonest of people to pretend a cordiality they didn't feel, simply because you were useful to them.

And then, as she turned back to that Nocturne with the pretty tune, the one in E Flat major, her mind completed its circle and came back to the grievance of the morning. To think that they had both forgotten again. A word would have been enough. But nothing from either of them : it was too cruel.

And then she suddenly shut up the Chopin and rose from the piano-stool. At least, though others failed to remember, she could make a little occasion for herself : a lunch in town and perhaps a concert. She went into the dining-room to search *The Times* for concerts. What luck ! There was a Pachmann recital that very afternoon at the Queen's Hall : the concert of all others that she would have chosen. She rang the bell. " Mary, please tell cook that I shall be out for lunch." Then she went upstairs and dressed herself carefully. Her champagne silk, she decided, and the hat with the fluffy fawn-coloured feather which always gave her profile, she thought, a peculiar distinction. But

whom should she invite ? Mrs. Rimington ?
No. Mrs. Rimington was so eccentric, so apt
to say things that she could not understand,
though she felt uncomfortably that they were
meant to be witty. And then there was Mrs.
Parke. But Mrs. Parke talked so much that
you never got a chance of saying anything at
all. No, she did not feel inclined for Mrs.
Parke. Miss Vansittart ! Why, of course, Miss
Vansittart would do perfectly. And she dressed
well, too ; that was a consideration.

She reached Miss Vansittart's at twelve thirty.
Miss Vansittart greeted her with a gentle surprise.
Mrs. Hetherington had never called on her in
the morning before and indeed had never shown
her any special friendliness. Would she lunch
in town with Mrs. Hetherington ? Yes, she
thought ! . . . Yes, certainly ; she would be
delighted. " Just a little lunch by ourselves,
you know ! " said Mrs. Hetherington, " in
some quiet restaurant " : and when Miss Vansittart was ready they went off together in a
taxi.

It was certainly an excellent little lunch.
Miss Vansittart knew good food and good
service when she saw them, and both, on this
occasion, were beyond reproach. And Mrs.

Hetherington had insisted, though Miss Vansittart had at first refused, on a bottle of wine,
"just a small bottle of white wine." And very
good white wine it was : you are not likely to
go far wrong with Hock at seven-and-six the
half bottle.

But all the while, as they sat at their table for
two in a corner of the quiet, expensive restaurant,
Miss Vansittart felt puzzled. Why was it that
Mrs. Hetherington had suddenly become so
friendly ? She felt slightly uncomfortable too :
it was so strange to find oneself suddenly *tête-à-tête*
with a woman of whom, though one had known
her for years, one had always known so remark-
ably little. Mrs. Hetherington too seemed just
the least bit embarrassed. Their conversation
had its perilous moments : it seemed once or
twice that they had really nothing at all to say
to one another. But towards the end of lunch
Miss Vansittart's heart warmed towards Mrs.
Hetherington : she was not actually so uninterest-
ing as she had always supposed and the idea of
this little lunch was really very friendly.

Unhappily Miss Vansittart had an engagement
at half-past three, so Mrs. Hetherington went
to the Pachmann concert alone. And, after all,
it was better to go alone. Alone one could

64

simply give oneself up unrestrainedly to the music : and for two hours she sat, giving herself up. Even in the intervals she was too absorbed, too tearfully delighted, to do anything but occasionally to put her handkerchief to her nose or raise a hand to make sure that her hat was straight : and when it was over, she went home deliciously, ecstatically sad, enfolded in a rosy mist of Chopin.

And Faidie and Louis, delighted to discover that the mood of mysterious reproachfulness had vanished, were nevertheless puzzled by the air of triumphant independence which she main-tained towards them for the rest of the evening.

Mrs. Symington at Home

A NOTE ON THE BEHAVIOUR OF CERTAIN OF THE HIGHER MAMMALS

FOR TWENTY YEARS LADY BERTHA Foxley and the Honourable Mrs. Burnett had ruled over the society of their countryside. They had married for money rather than rank, for they knew that marriage without money is perfectly impossible and, after all, when it came to rank, each knew that she had enough for two.

Unhappily, Lady Bertha and Janet Burnett had quarrelled. The quarrel was, of course, notorious : no event of that importance can pass unperceived in a cathedral town. Thenceforward it would have been better to break all the Ten Commandments at once than to invite Lady Bertha and Mrs. Burnett to the same party or even to allow them to be exposed to one another by accident. On one terrible occasion the two ladies had called simultaneously on a common acquaintance, and their distracted hostess had only just succeeded in averting disaster by the deft manipulation of a French window and two (luckily she had two) drawing-room doors ; after which she had gone to bed spiritually serene (it is true), but physically prostrated.

But Mrs. Symington was different ; she was what is called a go-ahead person. When her husband bought a charming little property a mile from the town, she promised herself that she would, as she put it, " wake these people up." The quarrel between Lady Bertha and Mrs. Burnett was just what she wanted. " Take care to keep them apart ? " she said scornfully. " Nonsense ! I shall invite them together." And, what is more, she did.

The news caused excited consternation. It is safe to say that everybody except the belligerent ladies knew about the plot and, of course, everybody accepted with the greatest pleasure Mrs. Symington's invitation to her " At Home."

Mrs. Burnett was the first to arrive. Her entry caused a flutter, for every one felt that the curtain, so to speak, had risen.

Mrs. Symington received the great lady with becoming effusion, and Mrs. Burnett was already seated on a sofa with a cup of tea when Lady Bertha was announced. It was a great moment. Would the ladies make a scene, would they simply ignore one another, or would they treat

one another with elaborate and acidulated polite-
ness ? The company felt the same delightful
sensation as when something slightly profane or
indecent has been said. Half of them watched
Lady Bertha and the other half Mrs. Burnett.

What happened, however, was the totally
unexpected. Lady Bertha, with a sudden little
cry of pleasure and surprise, sailed straight for
Mrs. Burnett, who welcomed her with transparent delight.

" Dear Bertha," she said, with a charming
smile, " do come and sit by me."

The situation was over. The buzz of conversation was resumed, and the two ladies sat
smiling on the sofa and monopolized one another
for the rest of their visit.

" An unexpected . . . pleasure, Bertha," said
Mrs. Burnett. " What ages since we have
met ! "

" Since we have met, yes ; but not since we
have seen one another. I saw you only a week
ago, Janet, walking past the new Bank Buildings.
You appeared to be quite absorbed by them."

" Indeed ?   What can have been the reason ? "

" What, my dear, but your profound interest
in architecture ? "

Mrs. Burnett accepted the explanation with a

smile. " One sees," she said, " so little to attract one here. Your health, I hope, is better ? "

" Better ? Excellent, thank you, and has been for years."

" I am glad. I thought, of late, that you had been looking ill, or not ill, perhaps, but —in a way—older."

" What can you expect, my dear Janet ? In three years I shall be fifty. Tell me, does it not feel dreadful to be fifty ? "

" Age is a question not of years but of constitution."

" You encourage me. So one can slowly become accustomed to it ? "

" Your husband, I hope, is well, and more free to enjoy himself nowadays ? "

" Nowadays ? My husband left the city fifteen years ago."

" Indeed ! I had forgotten. I thought his constant visits to town were on business."

" You thought so, perhaps, because he often goes up by your husband's train. Why don't you insist on that poor man retiring ? Such hours at his age must be a great strain. But then—er—grocery, isn't it ? Such a tie, such a responsibility ! To keep the sand out of the sugar must in itself . . ."

"Dearest Bertha ! As witty as ever ! But your memory is not what it was."

"I have a better memory than you think, my dear."

"Yet you speak of grocery. My husband, as you well know, is on the Stock Exchange. Surely you are confusing him with some of Mr. Foxley's relations ? "

"My dear Janet ! Of what will you accuse me next ? I have never allowed myself to make fun of my husband's family."

As the contest proceeded, the two ladies found not only their wits sharpening but their hearts warming under the invigorating give-and-take. After a particularly smart slap from Mrs. Burnett, Lady Bertha could resist no longer.

"Dearest Janet," she exclaimed, "there is no one to compare with you. How absurd that we should be separated. Why, one has almost forgotten how to talk ! Promise me that you will dine with us on Thursday ? "

"Of course we will," replied Mrs. Burnett ; "that is, if my husband can get away from his grocery."

Lady Bertha laughed softly.

To their observers the two ladies had appeared to be conversing with the most perfect affability.

Smiles, inclinations, little brief gestures, pointed to an agile and amiable progress over the surface of things. Some asserted that a reconciliation had been effected previously ; others that the quarrel had been exaggerated. But Mrs. Symington maintained that she and she alone had done the trick.

So she had. But she had simultaneously done another of which she was not aware.

Lady Bertha and Mrs. Burnett easily divined that their meeting was the result not of ignorance, but of impertinence, and they agreed that Mrs. Symington was an intrusive and rather vulgar little person who must immediately be dropped. Thenceforth Mr. and Mrs. Symington ceased to count in the society of that countryside.

The Pursuit of the Swallow

AS EVERY ONE KNOWS, THE COLlege of The Open Eye in Babylon was founded by the Emperor Nabu, in whose reign science may be said to have begun. From earliest childhood this enlightened prince was a person of character. Even his manner of asking for more milk was distinctive, for he would thump his little fist upon the table and bawl out : " Ho there ! Another pint of milk ! " And, as the terrified slaves ran to obey, he would add over his shoulder : " And let it be an Imperial Pint."

Matters did not improve with time and his professors found themselves confronted by a very disquieting pupil. Not that he was idle. Quite the contrary : he was altogether too profoundly interested in knowledge. He absorbed in days what other children take months to learn, and called into question what other children eagerly accept.

Now before the foundation of the College of The Open Eye, scientific knowledge in Babylon was held to be complete, for it was stored up in the Sacred Books of Science and was not dependent on the errors of human observation.

From the Sacred Books the Imperial Professors derived their knowledge ; never from personal investigation. Indeed the Professor of Botany was in the habit of boasting that he had never seen a living plant. Such were the Professors who provided education for the young Prince.

The Professor of Botany taught him the description, government and virtues of plants. " Chickweed," he said, " is a fine soft pleasing herb, under the dominion of the Moon, whereas Cinquefoil is a herb of Jupiter and therefore strengthens the part of the body it rules. The Marigold is a herb of the Sun and under Leo. It strengthens the heart exceedingly and is very expulsive."

" And how is all this known ? " asked the Prince.

" Because," answered the Professor, " it is written in the Babylonian Book of Botany."

" But," objected the Prince, " you have told me nothing of Daisies."

" It is true," answered the Professor, " that we seem to see millions of these flowers carpeting our lawns : but daisies are not noticed in the Botany Book, therefore they do not exist."

" Then what are the small white flowers . . ." began the Prince.

"I do not know, Your Highness," said the Professor, "nor is it proper for us to inquire. It is wiser to take no notice of them."

"Then so much," answered the Prince, "for Babylonian Botany." And there, it seemed, the matter ended.

Similar was the Prince's initiation into Beast-lore and Birdlore. From the Professor of Beast-lore he heard of the Griffon which has the body and legs of a lion and the wings and beak of an eagle ; the crested Basilisk ; the Cockatrice , the Unicorn, and the Cheshire Cat.

"But you have taught me nothing of the Rabbit," objected the Prince.

"Rabbits," replied the Professor, "though we fancy that we see them daily both alive in the fields and dead in poulterers' shops, are not noticed in the Babylonian Book of Beasts. Therefore they do not really exist."

"Then what are the small white-behinded creatures . . ." began the Prince.

"I do not know," replied the Professor, "nor is it proper to ask. It is better to pretend not to see them."

"Then so much," said the Prince, "for Babylonian Beastlore." And there, it seemed, the matter ended.

74

From the Professor of Birdlore the Prince learnt of the Phœnix, which springs from the ashes of its parents, the Bombay Duck, the Pelican, which nourishes its young with its own blood, the Guttersnipe, and the Swallow, which spends the winter at the bottom of the Great Lake.

"And what about Sparrows ? " asked the insatiable Prince.

"Sparrows," answered the Professor, " which, it is true, seem to devour our crops in prodigious numbers, are, in reality, illusions. They cannot exist because they are not mentioned in the Babylonian Book of Birds."

"Then what are the little brown birds . . ." began the Prince.

" I don't know," replied the Professor, " nor, I fear, ought we to inquire. We can only be certain that, whatever they are, they are not Sparrows."

"Then so much," said the Prince, "for Babylonian Birdlore." And there, it seemed, the matter ended.

But there, in point of fact, the matter had only just begun. The Prince, it turned out, had profited by his education only too thoroughly, and one of his first acts after his accession to the throne was to call together the Imperial Professors and speak to them as follows :

"We see what we see : the rest is with the gods. The Sacred Books of Science will henceforth be under the priesthood and their contents will no longer be divulged to the uninitiated. But for the uninitiated we shall institute a system of profane learning and a new college called the College of the Open Eye, in which all of you, once Professors of the old science, shall be Professors of the new science.

"Now, in order that the new science may not be a wild shoot with no root in the ancient order of things, we are resolved to graft it on to a single fact from the old science. The fact that the Swallow hibernates beneath the waters of the Great Lake is, in the old science, a fact stated but not demonstrated. As a beginning, our new science shall prove this fact by the process of human demonstration.

"Now as to method. According to the old method, the facts were already provided and had only to be memorized : but in the new, the facts will have to be discovered by observation and classification. Thus, the Professor of Botany will study the growing plant, the Professor of Birdlore the living bird, while the

76

Professor of Beastlore will cease to peruse picture-books and will seek out the Lion in his den."

Without delay the College of the Open Eye was inaugurated, with the Emperor himself as Master and Director of Studies, and immediately the study of the hibernation of the Swallow began. The Professor of Birdlore was to be seen daily climbing about upon roofs or slung up to the eaves in a basket, watching the behaviour of the Swallow, or scouring the country with a butterfly-net in the endeavour to capture specimens for close study.

Meanwhile, other Professors were observed to be dredging mud and weeds from the bed of the Great Lake, or tremulously bearing home samples of lake-water in teacups, or seated in punts earnestly dangling fishing-rods, all with the object of discovering what there was about the lake which induced the Swallow to spend the winter in it. And the work went on apace, for the Emperor as Director of Studies instantly ejected any Professor found idle during working-hours, saying : "Away to the punts ! " or "Out you go among the Duckweed ! " In this way the Professors collected a vast store of information, for they found that their inquiries

77

led them inevitably into every conceivable depart-
ment of science. Yet, though they analysed
lake-water, pored over mud and waterweeds,
and grew extremely intimate with fishes, they
seemed to be as far as ever from solving their
problem. But the Emperor was not discouraged.
"There is nothing for it," said he, "but to
examine the bed of the lake in person and so
to take the Swallow in the very act of hibernation."

Then, early on frosty mornings, folk beheld
the amazing spectacle of bearded Professors
shuddering in bathing-drawers upon the brink
of the lake in an agony of indecision. But the
Emperor himself strode about among them,
aiding their indecision by means of a stout cane,
"for," said he, "am I not Director of Studies?"
So the Professors sprang into the freezing water
and the lake closed over them. And when
human nature could stand it no longer, they
emerged like gaunt diving-fowl, and the Emperor
asked them : "Well, and what about the Swallows?" And the Professors, when they had
regained their breath, replied : "Alas and alas,
Sire, we have failed in our quest."

"Failed?" growled the Emperor. "And
how?"

"Because," answered the Professors with chattering teeth, "though we have completely examined the bed of the lake, we have not found a single Swallow."

"Then," said the Emperor, "draw the proper conclusion." But the Professors continued to chatter their teeth and none dared to draw the proper conclusion.

Then the Emperor relented. "Surely," he said, "the proper conclusion is this : that, except in a highly symbolical sense (which does not concern us), Swallows do not hibernate in the Great Lake. Dress yourselves, Gentlemen, and hasten home to hot toddy and mustard baths."

That evening, the Professors were summoned to the Imperial Dining Table. The Emperor showed himself infinitely affable, and after they had eaten of a thousand meats and drunk of a thousand wines, he pronounced the following after-dinner speech :

"This, gentlemen, is a great day in the annals of the Empire. By your labours (assisted a little, perhaps, by my encouragement) you have delivered the captive from his captivity, the coward from his cowardice, and the sluggard from his sloth, and have set up a noble monu-

79

ment upon the path of human development. Continue, gentlemen, as you have begun (indeed, I am resolved that you shall so continue) and by your means the spirit of man shall be everlaſtingly renewed."

The Professors, much surprised and puzzled, cheered loudly as, looking back on the rigours of the recent paſt, they looked forward with the greateſt disquietude to a ſtill more ſtrenuous future.

The Defensive Flank

THE TIRED SOLDIERS SAT IN OR about the crumbling trench, far behind the advancing line, where the Company, after coming out of the attack, had spent the laſt two days awaiting orders. It had been, for some time before, a quiet front, and this trench, formerly the support trench, was provided at frequent intervals with wooden shanties and tin huts, some of which even ventured to the luxury of chimneys, so that its wavering and dilapidated length resembled the village ſtreet of some primitive tribe. Juſt behind it, a formidable array of batteries had been secretly eſtablished on the night before the attack, and four or five hundred yards in front of it the attack had been launched at dawn with a sudden tornado of artillery-fire, under which the earth leapt and shuddered as if at the ſtamping of a hoſt of giants ; the sky whined, hissed, and roared, and the crash of concussions smote the tin huts and wooden shelters in the support trench like the blows of enormous clubs.

But the wave of battle had swept far forward in the four days since the opening of the offensive, and now the place was deserted and quiet, except for occasional spells of shattering gunfire from the heavy batteries near by. But though life at the moment was quiet, their minds under a sluggish surface were restless and apprehensive, for they knew that the old days of routine —six days in the line, six in support, and six in some quiet green French village—days which now seemed to have been so restful, so comforting to the heart—were over. The future had ceased to be shadowy and remote, had suddenly grown imminent and terrible. No one knew now where he would spend the night, or into what appalling and fatal struggle he might find himself plunged at an hour's notice by the great, inhuman mechanism of warfare ; and the men waited, unhappily, drowsily, numbly expectant, their animal enjoyment of food, rest, and what in those times seemed comfort, continually transpierced by little stabs of dread which grew to a wide, aching sore in the mind whenever a Battalion-runner passed along the trench on his way to Company Headquarters.

Company Headquarters was a tin hut built into the wall of the trench, containing a bench, a table, and three wooden beds built one above the other like the bunks of a ship's cabin. Captain Journeyman sat there alone with his elbows

on the table and his temples between his hands.
He felt old, war-weary, and too listless to do
anything that had not, of necessity, to be done.
Purposeless thoughts, as if by mere gravitation,
flowed sluggishly along the channels of his mind.
The wreckage and desolation which, with brief
respite, had been his daily surroundings for two
years, had become a part of his brain—an endless grey background against which all pheno-
mena moved and vanished. And now, as his
thoughts grouped themselves of their own accord
into a vision of life as he had seen it during
those years, that rolling expanse of sodden,
livid, shell-pitted country became in his mind a
diseased and dying body through which the
endless network of railways, roads, hutments,
and trench-systems sprawled like blood-vessels,
arteries, and veins. And the blood that filled
them, that pulsed along their channels, that
wasted and was remade, was the ceaseless tide
of soldiers that flowed from the beating heart
of England across the Channel, along the interminable railways and roads, up the long
communication-trenches, to fill the lines with
ardent, suffering life, or broke in wave after
wave of feverish and agonized energy over that
numbed expanse, fell and were swallowed in the

churned clay, or shrank back thinned, wasted, and exhausted upon the pulsing vessel that urged them forward. He pictured them as red, glowing lines and little nuclei of warm red life in the greying body of the land, and then the sense of their humanity, their brave and pathetic gaiety, their despair and helplessness and their complete dependence on him, came upon him with a poignancy that was almost unbearable. So many of them had passed through his hands in those two years. Each time they came out of battle many of the familiar faces had vanished and strange ones had gradually taken their place. Some of the latest arrivals were hardly more than children. Half-a-dozen sprawled about outside the door of his hut, smoking cigarettes, or sat doubled up, laboriously pen-cilling a letter home, waiting for the moment when he would lead them into another chaos of smoke and slaughter. A sentimental, purposeless longing rose in him for this large family of young and old children who depended on him as on a father and seemed continually to occupy his thoughts. They, for their part, thought little of him. They liked him, respected him, and knew that they could rely on him absolutely. " 'E's a queer old stick, but 'e's the right sort, is old Journey," they said : but they would have been surprised if they could have known the feelings towards them hidden under that laconic exterior. For them, he and the four subalterns were a race apart with fancy ideas of their own, except when under the stress of raids or battles the barriers between them thinned and vanished. Now, too, they were drawn together by the ordeal they had shared during the two days of fighting and by their common uneasiness as to the future.

So, in this precarious repose and isolation the hours passed over them, unmarked, undifferentiated, till evening came as a surprise to men who had long ceased to notice what stage the day had reached.

At the grey forlorn end of evening another runner passed down the trench, and, immediately after, the two subalterns and all the sergeants were summoned to Company Headquarters. The order to move had come. At once the idleness changed to feverish preparation. From holes and shelters men swarmed into the trench. Sergeants and corporals pushed through the crowd, urging them on. There arose a babel of voices. "Come along with that Lewis Gun there. Fall in here No. 3 Section. Now then,

get a move on with them panniers. Lorſt yer
gas-mask ? Well, bloody well find it again."
The crowd feverishly sorted itself out, their
minds seething with a thousand doubts and
queſtions. But the queſtions were soon solved.
They were going into the line to take over an
advance position which was held by night only
—a defensive flank consiſting of a series of
small poſts thirty yards apart. Immediately
before dawn they would evacuate the position
and move back to a point two miles behind
the front line. Some of them received the news
in silence, others with cynical gaiety. " Cushy
job for the troops. . . . Short and sweet :
only six hours in the line and iron rations from
Jerry all the time. . . . Daisy-pushin' jobs
goin' cheap. . . . What offers ? " And soon
the Company, with Journeyman in front, was
marching under a livid twilight through a silent,
featureless, shell-pitted waſte—the new country
over which the recent attack had swept like a
hurricane, leaving it charred and dead like a
desert of the moon—into a blank diſtance beyond
the bounds, it seemed, of created things. Somewhere in that diſtance, Journeyman refleſted
grimly, the chaotic, hardly endurable ſtruggle
was working itself out towards an end which no

86

one could foresee, and he saw himself and his men—leader and led alike—the victims of inexorable circumstance, as slowly and wearily they plodded along with the patient, mechanical hypnotic plodding of men who had suppressed all hope and all desire. He could feel the strain of their tired and burdened bodies behind him in the dark, and he ached in body and mind as he exerted himself to drag after him all that weight of human reluctance and weariness.

The march protracted itself interminably, and gradually each weary man resigned his body to its mechanical task as a part of the body of the company and withdrew within himself into his own little world of dreams till there came a check in the pace and a message was passed down from the front—" Keep to the right. Mind the shell-hole." And each man, emerging from his dreams to the surface of reality, awoke to the fact that the twilight had died, the visible world of space had closed in about him, and he was marching in darkness. A heavy silence oppressed the world. A tepid wind, carrying fine rain, fluttered in periodic gusts out of the void before them, damping their hands and faces, and passing away into another void behind them. Then a change : a new order. " Break up into sections." And immediately the mind of each section stirred apprehensively into a thin cloudy fume of unspoken questions, assumptions, awakened memories. Danger ? . . . Shelled area. . . . The road shelled after dark ! . . . Getting towards the line. . . . How much more of this ? . . . Sleep. . . . The next chance of a sleep . . .? Supper . . . warm fire . . . warm colours . . . Home, safety, talks over the fire. . . . And then dear faces, voices, heartrendingly clear over the immense gulf of this age-long other-life of the war, dawned, shone, and faded in those troubled minds.

Thereafter they marched in little groups like beads along the endless string of the road and under the slow, shambling rhythm of the march and the uneasy stillness of the night the shaken sediment of thought settled again into a numb passivity. On, on, a quarter-of-an-hour, half-an-hour, three-quarters : then, remote in the night, three muffled detonations shook the silence and again the sediment boiled up into awareness and hung suspended, keenly listening. A thin, liquid whinneying sailed up high above them, but as they waited tensely for the moment when it would grow into a dangerous, absorbing

scream, it thinned away far overhead in a high
arch of sound and three dull, rending explosions
broke out, miles behind them. After that, their
minds remained uneasily alert. Was that the
beginning ? Would the enemy shell the road ?
But their march continued uneventful. Only a
long-range artillery duel slowly and ponderously
awoke, intermittently building intersecting arches
of sound in the dark height above them—
rippling, whining progressions ; remote, hollow
rattlings like distant trains ; prolonged, hissing
flights, aloof, leisurely, monotonous—and then,
beyond either horizon, dull slow, sombre explosions like the dropping of enormous rocks into
a still, deep ocean.

All at once the front section became aware
of the nearness of human life, which defined
itself soon as movement and vague sounds in
either ditch ; and, peering downwards, they saw
a slit in the earth, receding at right-angles from
either edge of the road, in which, among a
swarm of dark and vaguely-moving shapes,
blurred white faces stared up at them. It was
the point at which their road cut the new front
line. A sense of secrecy, tension, vivid and
ardent life, rose from that thin seam of humanity,
throbbing like an artery in the numb and livid

desert. An officer and two men climbed up on to the road and exchanged whispers with Journeyman, and then, with the two men as guides, the Company moved forward again, section by section, into the darkness. The distant firing had died down. The scraping of feet on the road, the creaking of equipment and the subdued coughing and snuffling of burdened bodies hung about them like an aura of sound enclosed in a silence so dense that it seemed a material presence. And now great obstacles lay across their path—tree-trunks felled across the road from either edge by the retreating enemy, barriers too low to crawl under, too high to climb over, without an effort which for those vexed and weary boys grew, in the course of half-a-mile, to a nightmare which repeated itself with agonizing persistence. The wind had freshened. Overhead there was darkness no longer, but a roof of floating cloud shot with suffused pallor from a hidden moon. The last tree was passed, and now a high bank protected the left side of the road and produced a faint glow of reassurance in the mind of each section. But, too soon, the bank dropped and even the level ground fell away on either side of them till the road became an embankment which ran out into dark space, high and isolated, like a breakwater into the sea. And just as the sections moved out into the open, the moon swam into a clear pool of sky, revealing a dim, interminable plain padded with wisps of shining mist and illuminating the long grey snake of the road till each section felt itself suddenly stripped, exposed, shiningly visible for miles, as if perched on a high stage in brilliant limelight. It seemed to be a moment of impending disaster.

But nothing happened. No watchful machine-gun opened fire. The distance all round them remained bathed in misty silence and, led by the guides, they turned section by section down the bank on the left of the road where, following its line, short sections of trench like narrow graves showed faintly at intervals of thirty yards. Soon each section was quietly installed in its place, two sections to a trench—and the posts became small throbbing nuclei of life and awareness in the sodden waste of clay. In each the familiar routine began, the mounting of the Lewis Gun, the deepening of the trench, the flow of desultory, whispered conversation. Sergeant Hannet was busy in his trench with Sections 3 and 4. " Now, let's have a look at that Lewis Gun. That's right. Remember you've got to cover the gap between us and the chaps next door. Now then, you blighters, don't dig down too deep there : this ain't a game of 'ide-an' seek. What abaht the fire-ſtep ? We might feel inclined, later on, to fire a round or two, jeſt for fun. Sentries ? Lor' Lummy ! Everybody's got to be a sentry to-night. Some of you chaps don't seem to know what real war is : seem ter fancy you're in a nice, comfortable front line with a couple er belts er barbed wire in front of you. Suppose you'd like to get dahn to it till Jerry calls yer with yer early cup o' tea. . . . And remember, you chaps ; don't fire too soon. Let 'im get close an' then open up nice and ſteady and fire low. And then, juſt when 'e's goin' ter shike 'ands wif yer, a nice bomb or two popped in'ere and there, like rysins in a borf-bun.''

Under this flow of aſtringent conversation the men forgot their weariness and apprehension, the tougher among them warmed by its humour into facing all eventualities with a cheerful ſtoicism, the more timid charmed by its lightheartedness and humanity into feeling that where a man could talk like that nothing terrible could happen. The time was even passing quickly. Quite soon it was half-paſt eleven, and ſtill silence surrounded them like a sea, unbroken except by distant and ominous detonations at rare intervals, or the far-away knocking of a machine-gun mocked by the ghostlier echo ; and still not a shadow stirred on the grey plain or among the wisps of thin moon-coloured vapour.

Then, quite suddenly, about midnight, a salvo of distant guns and in the air a rattling hiss of shells, a hiss that grew to a roar that seemed to be descending full upon them. They cowered in their narrow trench and crashing explosions behind and before them made the earth leap like a great body. In the silence that followed, clods of turf came thudding to the ground and fragments of metal hummed past over their heads. " Iron rations," said Sergeant Hannet laconically, and whispered conversation filled the trench.

" What were those ? Five-nines ? " " Five-nines, I don' think. You'd soon know if a bleedin' old sank-nerf come over. Them's four-twos." " A nice quiet thing, a four two ! Not even as bad as a whizz-bang. You know when 'e's comin', an' a whizz-bang's come before 'e's started, so to speak : that's what's the matter wif 'im. . . ." " Is that the issue ? " " Some 'opes. There'll be a bit more to come yet, I reckon."

And more came, filling the night with fire and drifting smoke, tearing great holes in the earth, and with them, slower, heavier shells, rushing earthwards with an even more menacing roar and bursting behind them on the road and beyond the road with a long, rending crunch like the tearing asunder of great rocks. And crouching in their trench they waited patiently, with a good heart, for the ending of it. Only when a shell burst so close to them that they caught the hot flash of it, were wrapped in thick smoke and the terrifying stench of fire, when the trench that held them rocked like a loco-motive, a slow, white, smarting fear opened in their vitals, like a physical disease. It was the body, face to face with death, protesting against mutilation and destruction. Then, as in a rain-storm, they felt or seemed to feel a slackening in the onslaught . . . then a pause between two shellbursts . . . another, that grew and grew unbelievably, beyond all hope, to a blessed silence. The whole world, as on the morning after a hurricane, breathed silence, peace, and refreshment. They rose stiffly from their cramped positions and stretched themselves, inhaling the clean night air. A dark shape stood above them. " Everybody all right, Hannet ? " said a quiet voice.

" All right, sir."

" Good. Only about three hours more, you fellows " : and the shape faded out like a ghost.

The trench broke into whispers again. " Who was that ? The Skipper ? Rum old card. Strolling about regardless. Pleasant evening for a stroll : not 'arf. Remember 'im at Bullecourt ? Time we was lyin' abaht in shell'oles bein' shelled to bloody 'ell ? Moonin' abaht, 'e was, wif 'is map an' 'is bloody fieldglarses . . . seemed ter fink 'e was at a bleedin' rice-meetin'. ' Can yer see B Company on the left, Corporal ? ' 'e sez ter me. Now I arsk yer, 'ow could I see B Company when I was busy burying me fice in the mud. D'yer remember 'im at Armenteers, Sarge ? " A dull, spasmodic rumble broke their chatter. The sky narrowed to a core of shrieking rage, falling upon them headlong, swallowing them up till it burst like an express train out of a tunnel, and, huddled at the bottom of their trench, they gave themselves up, lost their identity in a shattering chaos of fire and darkness, volcanic explosions, showering earth-clods and the scream and hum of flying fragments of steel.

And when, after half-an-hour, another short respite came, no one spoke. Their energy was exhausted. Like men who had come through a long and dangerous illness, they were tired and weak and hungry. Their only thought was to hold out till the hour of escape ; and with all thought obliterated, with minds closed and battened down, oblivious of the passage of time, and dimly aware only of the coming moment of release as of a faint spark of light at the end of a long tunnel, they submitted themselves again to the inevitable ordeal of the bombardment. . . .

And quite suddenly, it seemed, an empty grey distance had opened out in front of them. A steady wind swept the sparse, wiry grass which hissed towards them like a spent wave. It had grown suddenly colder. They shivered, feeling like grey, bloodless creatures without vitality, and looking up, they saw that overhead, too, there was no longer darkness, but an empty vault of grey, more desolate and lifeless than the blackest night. The shelling had stopped again—died, it seemed, as a man might die, from mere exhaustion. Footsteps shuffled on the road behind them, and a flight of dim figures hurried away down the road. The moment had come. The shape of Journeyman strode towards their trench. " Get your men out as quick as you like, Hannet, and make for the sunken road," and he hurried off to the other posts. Sergeant Hannet scrambled out of the trench. " Now, you first, Corporal," and reaching down, he hauled the Corporal up. " Off you go, an' look out that the chaps follow you. Next man ! " and he hoisted out another scrambling fellow, and pushed him off after the Corporal. How slow they were ! Stiff with cold and cramped with long standing in the narrow trench, burdened with their equipment, rifles, and Lewis Gun, each man seemed to hang back deliberately. It was all he could do to control his temper. " Come along, now. Come along. Get a move on. Some of you chaps want a wet-nurse to look after you—somebody to wheel you 'ome in a blarsted pramberlater."

They ran stiffly, struggling bent and breathless against the furious wind—a straggling line of curved, tottering shapes following the Corporal. But Sergeant Hannet was still hoisting out the last men when the shelling opened up again. They ran, stumbling and recovering, the wind roaring in their ears, until above the shriek and roar of the wind came the shriek of the dropping shells, and they fell on their faces and the storm burst among them with the crashes of imminent thunder. Hard on the crash they were up again, running and dropping in their enthralled race for safety. Soon the first of them had reached the sunken road, and by degrees the noise of shellbursts grew less formidable, thinned, and lost substance behind them, and the gasping men slackened their speed. . . .

Before long they had crossed the front line and were marching, formed up into sections, back, back, into the calm and safety of the land behind the line.

And within two hours they were resting under a row of tall poplars whose showers of yellow leaves soothed them with a soft watery hiss in the heavenly calm of an October sunrise. Some of them lay at full length with equipment thrown off, staring up into the hanging domes of yellow, shimmering foliage ; others watched with a glowing contentment the smoking cookers round which the fatigue parties waited to carry away the breakfast for each company. And among the business and excitement of breakfast, and the good, steaming tea-dixies, they laughed and chattered like a swarm of birds, swallowing the blessed food and drawing in with deep breaths the delicious peace which hung visibly over them in the gold of the morning.

Captain Journeyman stood watching them. His weary, cynical mind recognized in his own body the customary reaction from unendurable strain—the sense of animal contentment and well-being which he received thankfully but without illusions. There was nowadays a bitterness at his heart which no bodily or mental relief could soothe, and even while he felt himself cheered and warmed by the glowing contentment of his breakfasting children, he could no longer resign himself wholly to the living. Half of his mind lingered among the thirty dead men whom he had found scattered along the defensive flank, as he ran from post to post in the tail of the running sections.

* * * *

Sergeant Hannet's party had joined the rest of their platoon and under the stimulus of food and hot tea their spirits rose. They eased their young minds in gay chatter of the oppression of a night which already seemed strangely remote. But Sergeant Hannet himself was not there. He was lying carelessly and comfortably two miles away, near his trench, with one arm flung wide and a round, irregular hole in his forehead. His face was grey-green like a hollow wax mask, his eyes half closed like the eyes of a dead bird, and a fly that gleamed in the sunlight crawled in and out of the hole in his head.

Escape

ROBERT SAT ON A GARDEN BENCH in the sunshine watching his wife with a sort of despairing admiration as she moved from rose-bush to rosebush snipping off the dead blooms and thinning out the small green buds where they were too crowded. He had hoped that their month's visit to this cottage in the country might produce some change in her and that somehow—exactly how he had not reasoned out —they might relapse into their old happy rela-tion. And yet, he asked himself with a sinking of the heart, had they ever really been happy ? Even when they were engaged to be married she had always been elusive, undemonstrative, seeming to feel little more than a good-humoured tolerance of him, and he had been harassed even in those days by the fact that he must perpetually restrain himself, never allow himself any express-ion of the infatuation which possessed him. But that, he argued, was his fault, not hers. She was such a refined, ethereal creature with emotions so sublimated that they showed them-selves, if at all, as a succession of delicate lights and shadows. That was why he loved her : she was such a contrast, with her restraint and her beauty, to his clumsy, torrential self. And she had loved, too, to listen to his talk. He used to set himself deliberately to attract her ; he got to know exactly what sparkling effects to produce in order to catch her fancy ; and when sometimes he achieved the final triumph of breaking through her last defence, when her face suddenly lit up and she threw back her head in a burst of that delicious laughter which he so rarely heard, a glow of estatic contentment took possession of him and he felt for a moment released from his continual restraint. But it was not even then complete release, for to do as he felt impelled to do, to seize her half playfully, half passionately, in his arms and overwhelm her with a burst of comical, tender, bantering talk, would have driven her back in a moment into her sanctuary. Still, after they were married, he had always assured himself, she would grow out of her fastidiousness. Each would enrich the other : she would gain something of his warmth and expansiveness and he would learn from her to be less clumsy, less wholesale in his talk and behaviour.

But, as it turned out, nothing of the kind had happened. On the contrary, soon after their marriage she had shrunk away from him still

farther : his passion for her seemed to oppress
her, and it oppressed him too, for as she retreated
from him both in mind and body and ceased at
laſt even to relax at his amusing talk, it hung
upon them both like a ſtorm-cloud that never
breaks, but holds the day from morning to evening under an uneasy, thwarted expeƈtancy.   No,
they had never been at ease from the beginning,
he owned to himself now, as with a weight at
his heart he watched her bend with an exquisite
unconscious tenderness to rescue a bee from one
of the over-blown roses which she had juſt
dropped from her scissors.   Lovely, tormenting,
inaccessible creature !   It was impossible, obviously and hopelessly impossible, he told himself,
that with his too-much and her too-little, they
could ever find a mean of contentment.   Juſt as
before their marriage his hope that married life
would solve their dilemma had been futile, so
lamentably futile, he now realized, was this new
hope that a month in a country cottage would
help them.

   And had he ever really hoped it ?   Was not
his real motive in taking the cottage—a scheme
to which she had at firſt objeƈted and then
liſtlessly assented—simply to get her to himself,
away from those unknown diſtraƈtions which in

London kept her so much away from home and tortured him with agonizing questions which he never dared to put to her ?

For a moment he realized the truth that to force her thus into close contact with him was, if he wished to retain any hold over her, the worst thing he could have done. Yes, to leave her free was the only hope : yet the fear that if he loosened his hold she might drift away from him completely was too much even for his perspicacity. His passion obscured his moment of reason : he dared not face the risk ; and like a drowning swimmer he hastened the disaster he feared by his very struggles to avoid it. The consequences of his step faced him already. Already in the two days that they had been in the cottage she had withdrawn herself farther from him, he reflected : and, as if to impress the reflection upon him now, she stopped her gardening, advanced towards the house up the stone-flagged path, and brushed past him without so much as a glance at the gaze of shy devotion with which he greeted her approach. The blue silk of her skirt caressed his hand and the touch of it sent a sudden wave of despair over him. It was an old dress, a dress which she had bought two years ago soon after their wedding, and the

touch of the silk reminded him vividly of something that he had never thought of since—of
how, on the day when she had put it on for the
first time for him to criticize, he had made a
transparent pretence of appreciatingly stroking
the blue silkiness of it for the mere delight of
touching her, while she, pleased and flattered,
had tolerated it with her half-contemptuous,
half-indulgent smile. The blue of that dress
was the dark blue of her eyes and when she
wore it her eyes shone with a richness and transparency strangely and fascinatingly alive in the
quietness of her black hair and pale face, transforming her into a creature still more tantalizingly
desirable and aloof. A pain that was almost
physical made him stir from his immobility on
the bench and draw a deep, tremulous breath.
Her he could not blame : that was perhaps the
worst of it. There was nobody, nothing he
could blame. The whole situation was simply
a desolating mischance. And yet even when
he told himself coldly and logically that they
were completely unsuited to one another, he
could not realize it, for his passion kept telling
him that she at least was all that he desired :
blindly, in spite of all mere reason he desired
her, and that surely was the supreme proof. No,

it was simply some little obstacle, like the grain
of sand that throws out the whole beautiful
machine, which spoilt him for her and left him
with his offerings of love, sympathy, and cheerful-
ness flung back at him unused as things distaste-
ful to her. He felt tired and dejected : the
whole of his bodily and mental life seemed to
be baulked of its natural expression and meaning,
and he looked, as he sat there crestfallen, like a
large pathetic dog with all its innocent pride
cowed by some opposition which it could not
understand.

Again she emerged from the house, carrying
a basket, and despite the instinct which urged
him not to annoy her with dumb beseechings,
he glanced up at her, for fear, just for fear he
should miss the blessing of some little glimpse
of kindness from her. This time she did glance
at him, but it was worse than if she had avoided
him, for there was a chilling apathy in her eyes.
She looked at him as she might have looked at
a wall, and in his bewilderment and despair it
became suddenly clear to him that this isolation
in the country might, after all, help them, though
not in the way he had anticipated ; for now
he realized from her quick reaction to the change,
that a crisis had become inevitable ; yes, and

not only inevitable but (however much he feared it) necessary, since the present tension was unbearable. Besides, the longer the crisis was postponed, the more difficult it would be, when it arrived, for them to speak unreservedly, since daily now new barriers were growing up between them. On their journey down into the country two days ago he had for the first time discovered the depth of her resentment against him for taking her from town. During the two hours in the train she had sat frozen by his side, answering him in monosyllables or not at all, and since their arrival at the cottage she had spoken to him (and then coldly, constrainedly and perforce) only at meals. They must have it out : yes, certainly, without delay. Yet, as she knew, she had only to ask : he existed, surely she knew, for nothing else than to please her, give her all and more than all she asked. But there suddenly he pulled up : could he, after all, give her everything ? Suppose she were to ask him ? . . . But she could never ask that. If once they could talk, all would be straightened out. But evidently it was he who would have to start : without a movement from him she would only lapse into a deeper and deeper silence. Yes, he must begin it, and obviously the sooner the better. He sat there absorbed, trying to accustom himself to the idea. Her steps sounded again on the path and his heart began to beat violently : terror assailed him. Not yet : he could not begin immediately. He must get himself into some sort of preparedness. And as she moved about the little garden, he sat there in a fever trying to muster resolution for the ordeal. Three times, four times she passed his seat, and each time his speech dried up and his heart dropped like a stone. The fifth time, he had spoken before he was aware of it.

"Marjory !" he said. She stopped. "Come and sit here. I want to talk to you." Coldly and obediently she sat down on the bench beside him. "Tell me," he began, "what is the matter ?"

"The matter ?" she answered in an even, expressionless voice. "Nothing. Why ?" She was gazing, her lips set in their cold, perfect curve, across the garden towards the hills that held their cottage and the other scattered buildings of the village like pebbles in a great bowl.

"Why indeed ?" he took her up. "Marjory," he began again gently, and laid his hand on hers. She drew hers away with a sharpness, an aversion, which cut him to the heart.

"And yet," he commented bitterly, "you say that nothing is the matter ?" There was silence. She could not, or would not, answer. "Wouldn't it be better for both of us," he went on, "to talk it out quietly and frankly ? Tell me why it is that you hate me so."

"I don't know," she answered moodily.

"You don't deny it, and yet you can't give a reason ?"

"No."

"Because I brought you down here ? Surely you know that if you had not agreed I should never have insisted ?"

"No, no," she replied, "it's not that."

"What then ? Little things perhaps that I do or say which irritate you. Tell me, my dear, and I'll try to alter them." She looked at him in his simple anxiety almost pitifully.

"Can't you mention them ?" he persisted gently.

"What's the use ?" she said wearily. "People cannot change themselves simply by wanting to."

"What can I do, then ?"

"Nothing," she replied with a sigh, half weary, half impatient.

He was infinitely patient. "But surely you

feel, Marjory, as I do, that we cannot go on
like this ? It makes you miserable and you
muſt see that it's torturing me."

" I don't do it on purpose," she began, as
though at laſt determined to speak. " I hope
you realize that."

" How then does it happen ? "

" I don't know," she went on desperately.
" It has grown slowly, by degrees. We should
never have married, Robert. It was my fault.
I never loved you from the beginning."

His heart dissolved like water. " But you
liked me," he said.

" Yes," she went on. " I liked you, and I
was flattered, like a fool, by your admiration :
but we were always different, hopelessly different."

" And now," he said, " even the liking has
turned to hate."

" Not hate," she said : " but you irritate me
continually. Oh," she added, " it's not your
fault, I know. There's nothing the matter with
you, Robert. But it's not my fault either : at
leaſt, I've had no choice. It has simply grown
on me, like a disease. I didn't want to dislike
you : why should I ? The real truth is that
we were always hopelessly incompatible."

His reason recognized the lamentable truth of

it even while his emotions and desires cried out
against it as monstrous. It was monstrously,
incredibly cruel that this creature whom he
desired with his whole body and soul should
be somehow unsuited to him, and his mind ran
off on schemes that might mend things. She
might go away, abroad, and have a holiday from
him ; or stay at home but, whenever she wished,
have her meals in another room and see him
only when she felt inclined ; or again, if they
were always outspoken with one another, avoided
all disguise and repression, might not that cure
their disease ?

But to all his schemes she opposed a determined refusal : she was resolved, it seemed, now
that they had succeeded in stripping themselves
bare of all disguises for one another, that the
final reality should be faced. Just as before she
had so resolutely shut herself into her exclusive
silence, so, now that he had wrested open the
door of escape, she was resolved not to stop
half-way. Freedom, she justified herself by
thinking, was as indispensable to him as to her,
and by confessing to the uttermost she could
give him that freedom and at the same time lay
bare her one deliberate deceit towards him.
And so when he pressed, poor fellow, for at

least a trial of his pathetic schemes, she inexorably shook her head. " It would be useless, Robert."

" But how can you tell till we've tried," he implored.

" Because, Robert "—she spoke clearly and deliberately—" there's some one else."

He understood at once : it was as though he had been waiting for it, and they sat for a moment of frozen silence. Then like one who has received a blow, he took his head in his hands. " Who ? " he asked in a voice unlike his own.

" What can it matter who ? " she asked, shaken for a moment at the sight of his grief. " Don't blame me too much, Robert," she went on, more humanly than she had yet spoken. " There was much that I couldn't help."

He felt her hand on his shoulder and heard her depart towards the house.

And so it was here at last ; all the cold unformulated doubts had suddenly materialized into this heartrending certainty. His mind was dark and empty. Misery, like a large hand, had closed over him and, looking desperately ahead, he saw no escape from it. The thought of such a future terrified him. He sat immovable for an hour, his face in his hands, concentrated like a wounded soldier, on the pulsing pain of his

wound. Then he opened his eyes and stared
at the things before him—faced their hard, cruel
reality, hoping foolishly that they would suddenly
dissolve into dream and take this unbearable
nightmare with them. But no : they were real,
terribly real : they stood there stubborn and
obdurate, beating on his flayed senses in all their
minute and remorseless detail : the glazed laurel
leaves with their alternation of shine and shadow ;
the hard, lurid red of a flowering dahlia ; the
earth beneath it on which a piece of broken glass
glinted beside a little brown stone. He stared
at them all in horror as though they bore for
him some sickening association. How should
he ever face dahlias and laurel again ? Then
his mind sought strange and hopeless escapes,
wove endless conversations, quarrels, explanations, all that he might have said to her, things
that could not have failed to win her back, happy
solutions in which the cloud was lifted and they
embraced in perfect understanding.

When next he looked outwards he was astonished to find that the sun had set. The garden
was very still : it was the moment before the
colour fades out of things. In the flower-beds
the whites shone cold and ethereal and the reds
smouldered with a last subdued richness. Some-

thing showed white on the bench beside him :
it was a cup of tea. She muft have brought it
out for him at tea-time. Tears rushed to his
eyes. He ftretched out his hand and touched
it : it was quite cold. Where had he been,
what had he been thinking about all this time ?
It was as though he had awoken from sleep.
His mind was clearer now—clear and cold like
the evening light. The pain was not less, but
now, it seemed, he could cope with it. He could
coldly, miserably, but rationally now, hold on to
exiftence till time and habit brought some sort
of alleviation. But what was he to do ? If he
went into the house he would meet her ; if he
ftayed where he was, she might come out : and
the thought of her, the mental picfure of her,
roused in him an irresiftible flood of tragic feeling. It was only, he suddenly became aware,
on condition of not seeing her, not even thinking
of her, that he could hope to preserve this sane,
passionless mood which was his only refuge.
Slowly and heavily he rose from the bench. He
felt as if, since he had sat down there a few
hours ago, he had passed through a long and
dangerous illness.

Darkness was falling as he quietly closed the
garden-gate and ftepped out into the road. He

walked ahead at a good pace : the physical
exertion and the rhythm of walking filled his
mind and kept out all else than a dull smart.
His senses were preternaturally keen. He saw
for the fraction of a second the silhouette of a.
bat—a spine-winged, headless bird—outline
against the clear green of the sky. He heard
the soft hiss of an unseen reed-bed and the
damp mossy perfume of sedge told of a brook
near by. From the black mass of a barn the
soft fragrance of hay waylaid him. Then again
he was lost to outward things and came to himself later—how much later he did not know, but
stars were now bright in a profound sky—to
find that he had again been absorbed into his
tragedy, involved in endless conversations, endless arguments. He must keep control of himself. Rigorously to banish it, to banish her,
from his mind was, he knew, the only way.
Suddenly he became aware that he was very
tired, exhausted both mentally and physically.
He had no idea how far he had walked. Now
he was climbing a hill : behind him lay the
valley drowned in a soft moonlit mist : before
him, to his right, loomed a mass of huddled roofs.
He climbed the hedge and approached them.
They were haystacks. Their sides bulged out-

wards from the ground, so that a man lying
against them would be sheltered. He pulled a
little of the hay out of one of them and made
himself a bed under its leaning wall. His legs,
eased of the weight of his body and the labour
of walking, tingled with a pleasant numbness :
the fragrance of the stack enclosed him like a
mist : the hay gently pricked the back of his
neck and his leaning cheek. . . . He sank and
sank, through clouds, through mounds of ver-
dure, through the wide boughs of leafy trees.
He lay on the floor of a forest, listening, watching. He was a hunter. Something white moved
among the tree-trunks. He held his breath. It
stepped out into a forest clearing . . . a white
stag with a white ivory horn, like a crucifix in
the middle of its forehead. It looked about
inquisitively with quick, elegant movements and
moved its pointed ears ; then, catching sight of
him, bounded away with an exquisite thorough-
bred grace into the trees. He sprang up and
dashed after it. Up steep slopes, down into
sudden valleys they ran. The stag flickered
before him among the trees like a white flag.
He came out into a clearing : the stag was
already half-way across it. He drew his bow
and let fly. There was a sharp, shrill yelp and

he realized that he himself was the stag and
what he was pursuing was Betty, the little white
fox-terrier which he had had as a boy. She ran
with her tail down and looked back at him
reproachfully with frightened eyes. He called
to her and she stopped and looked back at him.
Betty ? What had put Betty into his head ?
For a moment there was a blur in his mind,
and then all was clear again. Yes, the fair-
skinned Amazon looking back at him was certainly Betty : he recognized her unmistakably.
Again he called : " Betty, Betty ! " A flock of
Amazons ran transversely across the clearing and
sprang into the forest. Again he was running.
Up hills, down into steep valleys. The Amazons
flew before him with white, leaping legs and
hair that streamed behind them like golden
smoke. He could identify Betty among them.
She hung behind : she was panting, exhausted.
The others swept away from her and he caught
her up, caught her in his arms. He knew that
it was Marjory his wife. She returned his gaze
with those deep blue eyes of hers and a delicious
smile broke over her face. Suddenly her pupils
contracted : the smile narrowed into an expression of hatred, an expression which soon absorbed
her whole body into one furious, expanding hate.

He shrank beneath her as beneath some fearful ogress. She raised an arm and a sudden piercing pain shot through his heart. He lay on the ground alone with the spear in his breaſt. He was dying : quietly and comfortably bleeding to death. His blood enclosed him in a warm, deep pool. Anne, the nurse of his early childhood, walked quietly paſt with a basket on her arm. She glanced at him without surprise and said, over her shoulder : "That's right. That's right. You're getting on fine. There'll be water-lilies soon." And he himself felt that he was all right, that everything was right. He was clear, calm, transparent. Small ripples ran soothingly across his surface. The spear in his heart had broken out into branches and leaves which hung over him. He could feel their cool reflection sinking into his depths. The leaves swayed and hissed softly under a passing breeze, the reflected leaves shivered, and a shiver of grey ripples coursed through his watery being. He was cold—clear and cold . . . clear . . . clear. . . . He opened his eyes. It was already getting light. The dark wall of the ſtack loomed up on his left side. The chill grey air was sweet with hay : the earth and sky were cold, ſtill and dimly luminous. It was as though he lay embedded in a block of crystal. His mind cleared. He was cold, very cold and stiff, and memory at once leapt back to yesterday, bringing again the weight to his heart ; but with it there was also a remote, long-forgotten warmth, the old youthful holiday feeling. The strangeness of his being there under the haystack pleased him. The smell of the hay, the unearthly half-light of dawn, a sudden rustling and shuffling in the hedge of some waking bird or animal, reminded him of old walking-tours during the summer holidays : he felt the old feeling of oneness with all that lives and grows. From the next field came the stamping and the long snorting expiration of a horse. He got up and stamped his feet too, and, after setting his clothes to rights and brushing off the hay, climbed the hedge and jumped down on to the road. Down the hill, three black trees hung in a dream over a huddled farm whose tallest chimney was sending up a straight shaft of blue smoke. He resisted an instinctive impulse to search the valley for the distant village he had left. Somewhere there she would still be asleep, her face nestled into the pillow in the way he remembered so piercingly : and she would sleep for many hours yet. Only the farm people were beginning

119

to stir at this hour. But all that was over—
part of an irrevocable past. He stood there
with the whole world to himself, himself and
the woods, birds, and beasts. Drawing a deep
refreshing breath he turned his back on the
valley, excluding from his mind all that the
valley held for him, and continued the climb
uphill. When at last he reached the crest, he
stopped to gaze forward into the new world
that lay beneath him, a great sunlit panorama
of pastures, woods, valleys, farms golden with
harvest, and scattered villages, each clustered
about its grey Gothic tower. The bright,
heathery hilltop on which he stood was drenched
in September dew which shimmered like the
broken fragments of a rainbow under the flood
of sunlight which had just reached it.

Little Miss Millett

ON MY WAY BACK FROM MY WALKS
I frequently look in on John Calder. He
is generally to be found busy either at his desk
or in his garden, but he is always ready to
abandon the one or the other for a talk, and he
is the best talker I know. When I looked in
on him yesterday, however, he was neither
gardening nor writing : he was tidying out the
drawers of an old mahogany bureau. One of
the drawers was out on the floor with its contents
disposed round about it.

I have discovered, he said to me as I entered
the room, that I am getting old.

Indeed, said I, and how ?

By the fact, he replied, that I have begun
nowadays to go through old drawers and cupboards and tidy things up. I do it with no
object, but simply because the impulse forces
me to. Now I have not looked into this drawer
for . . . Lord ! It must be a quarter of a
century.

So I should suppose from the state of this
lavender, I said, taking up a bundle of stalks
from which all the flowers had fallen. And
these—I picked up another bundle of twigs

and powdering leaves—I cannot even tell what they were.

They were roses, said Calder, and they and the lavender came from little Miss Millett's garden. He sighed and, going over to the fire-place, dropped both the bundles into the fire. Then with the tongs he rescued the lavender for a moment and filled the room with a cloud of sweet-scented smoke, which thinned as we watched it and lost substance like a ghost, till nothing remained of it but the perfume.

Tell me about little Miss Millett, I said.

Ah! replied Calder, if you start me off on poor Rose Millett! And it will involve others also. I shall have, first, to bring before you my Aunts Emily and Janet who lived together after the death of Aunt Emily's husband until they themselves were separated by death. Never were two sisters more different. How shall I describe them? Aunt Emily was a work of art : Aunt Janet was a natural growth. Aunt Emily was the perfection of reserve and refinement : her very childlessness, I used to think, must be due to the fact that she was too refined to produce children. But she had a great charm and she was kindness itself, and a house arranged and governed by her was the most perfect house imaginable. She loved old china, old glass, old brocades and beautiful furniture, and her attitude towards her friends and acquaintances was the same as her attitude towards objects of art—in fact, it was as objects of art that she appreciated them, including even their shortcomings in her appreciation, for were they not the patina on the bronze, the tarnish on the brocade?

But Aunt Janet did not bother about art, though she loved music. *Her* concern was humanity and nature. Everybody loved her. She made friends with every one she met, and would labour tirelessly to help anyone who wanted help. The time left over from that she devoted to the garden, and her garden was lovely, for Aunt Janet as a gardener was what Aunt Emily was as a housekeeper. In character, too, she was the very opposite of Aunt Emily. There was no reserve about Aunt Janet : she was free, hearty and exuberant ; vigorous and impulsive alike in mind and body. That packet there contains several of her letters to me. They will help me in telling you the story.

When the Aunts went to live at Arleigh, which was within closer reach of town, I used to stay with them constantly, and the occupation in which I found each of them at the moment of my arrival there on my first visit remains in my mind as typical of their characters : for Aunt Emily was in the morning-room carefully mending the paw of a priceless green Chinese dragon, while Aunt Janet was in the kitchen bandaging the wounded leg of a fox-terrier which its owner, a little girl who lived in the village, had naturally in such an emergency brought to her.

It was during that visit to Arleigh that I caught my first glimpse of little Miss Millett. Her age then, as I afterwards learned, was twenty-six. At that time my Aunts knew little about her : they had met her perhaps twice or thrice ; but even then they were beginning to take a lively interest in her. I had returned from a walk a little late for tea, so that I knew, when I went into the drawing-room, that I should find tea already in progress. Then, as I opened the drawing-room door, and before I had entered, instinct told me that a stranger was in the room, and as I went in I was aware of a little pale figure—was it pale blue, or violet, or pale green ? I only know that it was pale and, as I felt, a little faded—nestling in a corner of a chair between the two Aunts.

That scene and its immediate context, as they exist in my mind, are significant of the strong and very special impression which Miss Millett must have made on me at that first encounter ; for I was astonished to discover, on looking back to that period in my diary to-day, that they exist in my mind in a form which bears very little relation to the actual facts. For my memory had set the scene in late September, and yet in my diary it is incredibly and irrefutably entered under the middle of May. And, stranger still, the walk from which, in my memory, I had returned to find Miss Millett in the drawing-room, was a walk I had really taken in October of the year before—a wonderful walk over moor-land and down long wooded slopes into an old dishevelled village. Mists blurred the distances, and the moors, my diary reminds me, still glittered in the warm afternoon with the morning dew which had discovered and delicately adorned hundreds of little spider-hammocks that flashed to and fro from grey to rainbow iridescence among the twigs of the heather. And those exquisitely delicate and transient webs ; the autumn air so warm in the sun, so sharp in the shadows ; the scent, farther down the slope where the tall trees dripped orange and scarlet, of damp leaf-mould, half-sweet, half-sour ; the mist scented with wood-smoke which, farther down still, brimmed the little village, where damsons, frost-nipped before they could ripen, lay in the road under their tree, and the belated dahlia-buds in the cottage gardens drooped among blackened foliage ;—all these lovely details, which I had recorded and long since forgotten, lived in essence in my mind as a sense of beauty prematurely nipped, of youth blossoming too late, of something lovely but unfulfilled, and the more lovely for its unfulfilment.

And even the scene in the drawing-room I have altered, I find—plucked it from its May into a late autumn ; for as I remember it, so clearly, so acutely, the late autumn sun falls through the windows in a long ragged splash on the wall, gilding the edge of a gold picture-frame, lighting rainbows in the cut-glass vases, discovering the lustrous red of a polished maho-gany table ; and in the luminous grey shadow at the other end of the room, near a vase of late white roses with drooping heads and petals ready to fall, Aunt Emily and Aunt Janet with the little ghost-like figure between them sit, as though frozen into a hundred years' sleep, round the pale silver of the tea-service. What a strange perversion of the memory, I thought to myself as I turned over the leaves of my diary ; and then, as I reflected more deeply, I came to see that it was not a perversion but, on the contrary, an exquisite accuracy by which the memory, free from the arbitrary divisions of time and space, could so associate and mould into a living unity things which are so perfectly related in spirit. Thus little Miss Millett lives in my mind, carefully and tenderly embalmed in these perfectly chosen visions of the past.

But when I begin to reflect more closely on Miss Millett, her personality gradually emerges in much greater detail : just as, after that first impression as I stood at the drawing-room door, the pale little figure materialized for me into something more complex. For when we were introduced and Miss Millett's eyes met mine, I was aware of that strangely contradictory impression which I was ever afterwards to associate with her, which was perhaps what always made me think of her as something unstable, something fitful and evanescent, something less than real. For one felt in her a curious mixture of dignity and awkwardness ; a natural dignity, perhaps, marred by shyness ; the pathos and helplessness too, and alternately the uncouthness, at moments

even the hardness, of a child ; and, most striking
of all, a bewildering alternation of youth and
age, so that one could not guess whether she
were a prematurely aged eighteen or a strangely
youthful forty. Was it the hair drawn back a
little too severely from the delicate temples
which produced an illusion of age, or the rather
old-fashioned hat pushed the least little bit too
far back on the head which gave a look of false
youthfulness ? Were her manners, sometimes
so curiously and refreshingly immature, those of
a girl who had not yet had time to acquire the
manners of a grown-up person, or those of an
adult who had been cheated, somehow, of the
opportunity. Whatever the facts might be, this
unusualness, this quaintness in Miss Millett had,
in the sum, an irresistible charm. One watched
her delightedly, as one watches a beautiful timid
animal, and found oneself, in talking to her, at
one moment addressing her as an equal, at
another falling into a protective manner as with
a child. But none of these attempts quite
capture the quaint individuality of Miss Millett.
She was not really like a child, or an animal.
No ; she was rather some elusive, fairy-like
creature with just the faintest trace of gnomish-
ness. I should not, I think, have been sur-

prised if she had vanished suddenly in a fit of quiet weeping or a soft ripple of laughter.

But though I have tried to convey my earliest impression of Miss Millett in some detail, I did not see much of her on that first occasion, for soon after I had entered the drawing-room she rose to go. When Aunt Janet tried to detain her, she seemed really alarmed. " Oh no, no really, thank you. I *must* go. Mamma will be expecting me " ; and she looked appealingly at Aunt Janet who, taking her arm, went out with her to the garden gate. Was it something I saw in Miss Millett's face or only my own fancy that made the mention of her mother seem like a threat of distant thunder, just the faintest rumble which frightened the fairy away ?

" Such a dear girl ! " said Aunt Emily to me when we were alone, " and so devoted to her mother ! "

" And, I suspect, rather a formidable mother," I replied.

" Formidable ? Ah, no, poor thing : very far from formidable. A complete invalid. She hasn't been downstairs for years. But it is beautiful to see her daughter's devotion to her. What the poor child will do when her mother dies I cannot think."

"You have seen Mrs. Millett?"

"Dear me, no. She is far too ill to see visitors. But I have heard her."

"*Heard* her, Aunt Emily?"

"Yes. She has a stick with which she knocks on the floor, poor thing, when she wants Miss Millett."

"And she knocks often for Miss Millett?"

"Yes, fairly often, I fancy. You see, Miss Millett insists on doing everything for her, so as to keep the servants away from her mother's room as much as possible."

"I should have thought," I said, "that such a complete invalid ought to have a trained nurse."

"They used to have a trained nurse," said Aunt Emily, "so Miss Millett told me, but she ended by deciding that a trained nurse didn't answer—that it was much more satisfactory to keep everything in her own hands. It really appears as if the child were so devoted to her mother that she could not bear to entrust her to anyone else."

Aunt Janet, as she told me in a conversation that evening, had already begun to investigate the case of Miss Millett, and her view, as usual, was entirely different from that of Aunt Emily. She had already laid her finger on that instability, that fluctuation of opposing qualities in her which I have already mentioned, and she had marked it down as a symptom of disease. She recognized its curious charm, she said, but the impression it produced on her was painful, just as the strange little habits and movements which a caged bird evolves for itself as a sub-stitute for the free instinctive movements of its wild state, are both charming and painful. " In fact," said Aunt Janet, " it is precisely her charm which is the matter with Miss Millett. Don't you notice how at once, at the first glance, one pities her and longs to help her : help, in fact, is what she unconsciously keeps asking for. Every look, every gesture, is an appeal to one —isn't it ?—to open the cage for her. Do you understand what I mean, John—Emily doesn't —when I say that for me little Miss Millett is a tragedy ? The charm of the creature she *is* only makes me more aware of the tragedy of her not being the creature she might have been. Which she might still be," Aunt Janet added, " if only I could get hold of her."

Aunt Janet had never been to the Milletts' house. Aunt Emily had paid the preliminary call for both of them, so that Aunt Janet had *heard* Mrs. Millett, like myself, by proxy only ;

but I was not surprised to find, on further discussion of the Millett problem with her, that she had at once fastened upon the knocking on the ceiling as an important clue. " It is not as though the old woman had knocked once or even twice during the short time Emily was there. She knocked four times, so Emily tells me ; four times, John, during the period of a first call, and Emily's first calls, I need hardly tell you, never exceed the length laid down by strict convention."

Thereafter the problem stood still for a fortnight, for we saw nothing of Miss Millett during that time, and with the small amount of data at our disposal it would have been idle for us to have discussed her—that is, for Aunt Janet and myself. Aunt Emily, of course, was not interested in discussing her. She would as soon have discussed her own priceless Nankin jar. For her, Miss Millett was not a problem : she was a work of art, a perfect and unique specimen which to alter would be to spoil. Besides, she would have thought it an impertinence to inquire into Miss Millett's private life. But though Aunt Janet and I did not discuss Miss Millett, we thought about her a good deal during that fortnight, I with little more, at that time, than an idle though kindly curiosity, but Aunt Janet, I am sure, with all the solicitude of her generous heart.

It was undoubtedly my curiosity and Aunt Janet's solicitude which finally drove us in the direction of Miss Millett's home. We did not mention to Aunt Emily that we were going there, because we had not confessed as much even to ourselves ; but the fact that we started off at once in that direction and after an hour's walk found ourselves actually passing the house was sufficiently convincing, and I was not at all surprised when Aunt Janet stopped as though struck by a sudden inspiration and asked, " Why shouldn't we call, as we are here ? " And so, of course, we called.

As we approached the gate I felt somehow that we were on the brink of an adventure ; yet not an adventure, but some delicate, poignant experience. I had the impulse to walk on tiptoe, as one has it on entering a church, as though this further advance into Miss Millett's personality were an unwarrantable intrusion. The house and garden were hidden from the road by a high privet hedge, and when I had pulled open the gate, grained and varnished and adorned

133

with metal spikes along the top, the appearance
of the place came upon me with a shock, and I
heard Aunt Janet give a little gasp. For the
whole thing was the very negation of Miss
Millett—little, pathetic, mysterious Miss Millett
who had seemed to us not quite of this world.
I glanced at Aunt Janet in the hope that she
would suggest a retreat. "You see!" she
nodded to me, as though the scene had proved
some point of discussion ; and, so far from
retreating, she made, round the right side of
the circular drive, for the front-door. The
drive surrounded a close-shaved grass-plot, in
the centre of which was a round flower-bed
flanked by other kidney-shaped beds, and all of
these were ablaze with scarlet geraniums and
yellow calceolarias, edged with blue lobelia—a
triumph of fierce, professional bedding-out. The
drive, too, was yellow—hard yellow gravel which
crunched and clattered under our feet. Behind
all this, the house rose square, symmetrical, and
slate-roofed ; its walls were clothed in close-
clipped ivy as in a jacket, which fitted faultlessly
round the windows and front-door : in every
window four inches of red blind hung mathemati-
cally adjusted, and four red steps led up to the
open front-door, beyond which was another door

adorned with stained-glass. We seemed suddenly to have stepped out of the country into a mid-Victorian suburb.

It came to me at that moment—young prig that I was—that we had found Miss Millett out : that the tender sympathy of the Aunts and my own interest had been provoked merely by her shyness and not by any real charm of personality, and I braced myself for the completion of our disillusionment, for the gradual exposure of the real Miss Millett in all her banality. I felt as Aunt Emily would have felt at the breaking of an exquisite bit of Dresden.

The drawing-room in which we awaited Miss Millett confirmed my worst fears. It was a gaunt room, a room in which one would feel chilled even on the hottest day. I was aware of prim, meagre pieces of shiny black wooden furniture against drab walls ; and of the curtains, upholstery and carpet I retain a depressing sense of drab, terra-cotta, and brown. I remember, too, a formidable marble clock like a tomb under a glass case on the mantelpiece. But there was not time to notice much before the door opened, only a little and ever so gently, and little Miss Millett came round the edge of it and fluttered towards us smiling and blushing.

"What a delightful surprise," she said, beaming at us and taking Aunt Janet's hand in both of hers. At the first word, the first movement, all my doubts vanished. One felt it at once—the charm, the pathos of the strange little personality. At her arrival, the ugly room was transformed, or rather, one forgot its ugliness, one forgot its very existence : one's attention became wholly taken up with Miss Millett. She looked different without a hat—younger, I thought at first— for a shaft of sunlight lit up a little transparent halo of stray hairs curling about her forehead, too short, perhaps, to be caught back with the rest. Then as she came forward out of the sunlight and one saw the delicate temples and the prim little bob of twisted hair on the back of her head, she did one of her quick, bewildering changes, and I decided that without a hat she looked older. In her own home, the touch of awkwardness which I had noted in her at Arleigh had left her, and she welcomed us and offered us chairs with a charming dignity.

I had quite forgotten Aunt Emily's story about the knocking when, after we had been talking for about a quarter of an hour, the first blows came. Though they were not immediately above our heads, they were loud enough to startle us. Little Miss Millett too looked startled : I caught in her eyes that same expression I had seen there when she had mentioned her mother at Arleigh, and, jumping up in the middle of a sentence, she asked to be excused and hurried from the room. But we had been alone for hardly five minutes when we heard her step on the stairs again and she hurried eagerly into the room, as though afraid that we might have escaped during her absence. "You must excuse my running away like that," she said. "You see, Mamma requires constant attention."

"And you have no one to help you ? " asked Aunt Janet.

"No, not now. I find it more satisfactory to do everything myself."

"Then you have already tried a trained nurse ? "

"Oh yes, several : eight altogether ! But . . . well, I found that none of them were suitable ; in fact, I had great trouble with them," said Miss Millett seriously.

"My dear," said Aunt Janet, rising to go, "I cannot imagine you having trouble with anybody."

"But you're not going," said Miss Millett anxiously, taking Aunt Janet's outstretched hand. "Oh please, don't go. I hoped you would both stay to tea." She was so obviously distressed that Aunt Janet acquiesced at once, and at that moment the maid announced that tea was ready.

"I hope you won't mind having tea in the morning-room," said Miss Millett, leading the way. "I have it there because I can hear better there when Mamma knocks."

The morning-room, one felt at once, was a pleasanter room. In fact, it was by no means irreconcilable with Miss Millett, and as one began to notice details there were obvious signs of what must have been her influence, for a Morris paper covered the walls, a cretonne—blue, grey and rose—adorned the sofa and easy-chairs, there was a piano with music on it, and a French-window opened on to a little patch of formal garden.

"What a pleasant wall-paper," said Aunt Janet, taking in the room in her usual breezy fashion.

Miss Millett looked a little alarmed. "Oh yes," she said ; "I chose that. But don't talk about it, please. You see," she whispered, turning a charming pink, "I did a dreadful thing. Last year, when the room had to be

re-papered, Mamma chose a paper which . . .
which . . . Well, I had set my heart on this
one and, without ever telling her, I ordered it
instead of hers. She would be terribly vexed
if she knew. And this cretonne : it is not the
one she chose. You won't mention it, either,
will you ! I know I oughtn't to have done it,
but, you see, my mother never leaves her room
—she hasn't done so for over six years—so I
felt that I might perhaps allow myself . . ."

"Why, of course, my dear child," exclaimed
Aunt Janet. "I should have done the same
myself."

"Everything else," continued Miss Millett,
still trying to justify these innocent sins, "I
have left just as it always was. I have never
disturbed the books "—she pointed to a bookcase near the piano—" except to clear the bottom
shelf for my own."

I longed to go down on my knees and examine
Miss Millett's private shelf. What should I
expect to find ? I should expect to find Jane
Austen and the early Fanny Burney, whom Miss
Millett would read, I felt, with a single mind,
and without any of that amused detachment
which adds so much to the delight of more
sophisticated readers. And Wordsworth would

139

be there, and Robert Bridges, Walter de la
Mare, and, I hoped, the poems and novels of
Hardy and the short stories of Henry James,
whose subtlety and fragrance were so much a
part of Miss Millett, however little she herself
would be able to savour them. What a wonderful dip that would have been into the personality
of little Miss Millett : what secrets, what new
aspects would one not have discovered, what
fresh problems would not those new aspects have
raised ? But Miss Millett was pouring out tea,
and I did not discover, then or at any other
time, the names in that row of treasured books.

In that room, Miss Millett had said, she
could hear her mother better, and there could
indeed be no two opinions about that, for hardly
had we received our cups of tea than three smart
raps overhead electrified us. At once Miss
Millett sprang up and, begging us to go on with
our tea, hurried in agitation from the room.
Aunt Janet pursed her lips but made no com-
ment. We both felt, somehow, that we owed
it to Miss Millett not to discuss the thing in
that house. But afterwards, when the events
of that afternoon irresistibly cropped up between
us, I found that Aunt Janet, like myself, had
been impressed not by the fact that an invalid

should knock on the floor but by the quality of the knocks themselves. They were aggressive knocks, the knocks of some one who, whatever her illness might be, had a will, and muscles, of her own. And what made them seem the more aggressive, the more vicious, was their effect on Miss Millett ; for they struck her like blows ; they shrivelled the free expression of her personality at the very moment when it was unfolding itself so attractively in her entertainment of us. It was painful to see how at each shock all those little awkwardnesses returned to her from which, the moment before, she had been so perfectly free. It was as though some one were to tread upon a flower or wilfully to frighten a small bird just as it was being coaxed into tameness.

But almost immediately we heard her foot on the stairs again, and she reappeared looking rather shamefaced. " Mamma asks me to say," she began, " that she regrets very much being unable to come down to entertain you, and hopes you will forgive anything that happens to be . . . not altogether as it should be, because it is difficult for her to manage things when she cannot leave her room."

" But, my dear," said Aunt Janet, " you have

looked after us perfectly. Tell your mother so from me."

When tea was finished, I asked Miss Millett if she played the piano. "A little," she said, blushing like a child ; and, when we asked her to play, "Oh, but I don't play anything that people care for. Only Bach !" Her face was pink and her eyes shone with apprehension when we had finally persuaded her and she sat down at the piano. She was so nervous that she could hardly play the simple prelude she began with. Her touch faltered, she played false notes, left notes out. But in spite of it, one felt rhythm and understanding, and she must have seen, when she had finished, how genuine our appreciation was, for when she began again (it was a three-part fugue this time) all nervousness had left her and she threw herself gleefully into the fugue, weaving the intricate pattern of parts, picking out a hidden detail as though with a thread of scarlet, dropping it to catch up others from the dark background ; and all with such rhythm, such balance, such fine gradations of tone that the absence of power in her playing seemed actually to add a subtle beauty to the music, as if one had surprised some exquisite fairy concert played on tiny instruments. And to watch little Miss Millett's absorption, the bright colour of her usually pale face, her busy confidence (all her shyness gone), Miss Millett blossoming, as it were, before our eyes, was an experience even more delicious than the music. And then, as though to exhibit in little the whole tragic situation, that fiendish old woman upstairs suddenly gave her three knocks again. All of us jumped violently. It is almost farcical now, as I look back on it—the spectacle of us three, reacting each time so obediently, so regularly, to the dreadful old woman's stimulus. But it was not farcical at the time, for its effect on Miss Millett was tragic. She stopped dead. All the youthful happiness had left her face, and instead there was dismay, weariness, humiliation. It was as though the old woman were purposely trying to make her ridiculous in the eyes of her friends. Almost before we had realized it, she had fled from the room ; but again she returned almost immediately. " Mamma was afraid I might be tiring you," she said, with something of the weariness of a child repeating a lesson. " She thinks you would like to see the garden."

" I should love to see the garden," said Aunt Janet ; " though I hope another day you will play to us again. You play quite admirably, my dear."

I was not surprised to find that the little formal garden which I had noticed from the morning-room window was another of Miss Millett's escapes. Like the Morris paper, the cretonne, and the bottom shelf in the bookcase, it was the secret assertion of her own personality, her small corner of holy ground in an unsympathetic world. How exactly appropriate to Miss Millett, as I conceived her, was that small garden. There were pinks—both pink and white—violets, and musk, and frail pink monthly roses already in bloom ; and the whole square, of course, was surrounded by a lavender hedge. Indeed, I had answered " Of course ! " when Miss Millett pointed it out to me, so inevitable, so perfectly symbolic of Miss Millett had lavender seemed to me. Aunt Janet asked many questions about this garden and, though it was only about four yards square, we lingered there, touched by Miss Millett's tremulous pride in it. That pride, so eager for sympathy, so pathetically out of proportion to the garden itself, produced in me an almost painful impression. It was charming and lovable, but also, somehow, feverish and unhealthy. The child's mind surviving in the grown woman was, one felt, a deformity, and it pained one almost as the sight of a physical deformity to see such eager interest, such trembling sensibility confined, restricted, concentrated on such tiny matters. It was not the thing itself, but all that the thing implied of starvation and repression.

Yet now, as my mind plays round the personality of little Miss Millett, as I struggle to recall her and to define her case, I see that I have analysed the impression wrongly. For her mind was not intrinsically childish : it was in a way a mature though not a very self-conscious mind, which was compelled by force of circumstances to express itself like a child. For the fact was that Miss Millett's mind had grown up, while her world, her field of activity, had not been allowed to expand correspondingly. That very instability which was so typical of her, that seeming fluctuation between youth and age, dignity and awkwardness, was a symptom of growth, but it was a growth obviously forced out of its natural current. No, her mind was not a child's : it was the warped mind of an adult. She had seen nothing of the world. She knew nothing, I believe, of such things as good taste and bad taste, of the vagaries of fashion,

145

of artistic standards. She followed her impulses without referring them consciously to any standard of values, never classifying her own preferences as good and her mother's as bad ; in fact, as I came to realize, she was not clearly conscious of her antagonism to her surroundings. It was as though, almost in spite of herself, some ghostly ancestor or some blind instinct were driving her to express these small revolts. She would never, I believe, have thought of asserting that the drawing-room furniture was horrible, that the bedding-out in front of the house was vulgar. She accepted these things without criticism as parts of her world, and, as parts with which she had all her life been in contact, she even loved them in a strange unæsthetic way, as we so surprisingly discovered later on, even while her instincts exercised themselves in inventing refuges from them.

When at last we took our departure, Miss Millett accompanied us out of the spiked and varnished gate and a few yards on to the common ; and when, after parting from her, we looked back, there she stood, where we had left her, under some hawthorn trees, a small, solitary figure waving its hand as though to friends departing after a long, delightful visit. Then

146

as she stepped out from the grey shadow, the sun again caught her hair, and encircled her head, as before, with a shining halo of fragile and fairy-like youth.

"You see," said Aunt Janet, when at last we lost sight of the little creature, " it is exactly as I said. The poor child is simply enslaved : and the question is, how to rescue her."

"But surely," I objected, "she might, to some extent at least, rescue herself, simply by engaging a trained nurse ; but she actually prefers, so she said, to do everything herself."

"Of course she does, poor little thing," Aunt Janet burst out ; "and can't you see why ? As she told us herself, she has already .tried eight nurses before she came to that conclusion. But it's rather extraordinary, isn't it, that out of eight not one should be suitable ? However, after what we have seen, this afternoon, there is not much doubt about the truth of the matter."

"That, in point of fact, it is the old woman herself who is unsuitable ? "

"Just so. It was not Miss Millett who sacked the nurses : it was the old woman. There would be, I am sure, incessant rows, and then a periodic explosion ; and when, after the explosion, the poor little creature ventured out to inspect the damage, it invariably turned out that the nurse had vanished and Mrs. Millett remained. If only," sighed Aunt Janet, " it had been the other way about. And so," she went on, " it is not difficult to see why poor little Miss Millett prefers to look after her mother herself. It is an ingenious device, isn't it, or the old vampire's. Physically, it is true, she is a prisoner, but morally she tyrannizes over the whole house, and she has imprisoned her daughter much more effectually and cruelly, because she has imprisoned her mind and will."

During the remaining days of my visit we talked much of Miss Millett. Aunt Janet was determined that something must be done for her. The best thing, of course—the impossible thing—would be to transplant her completely. Till quite late in their intercourse Aunt Janet believed that it was only necessary to uproot her bodily from the restriction and starvation of her home life for Miss Millett at once to blossom like the rose. Not that she deluded herself with the idea that this was immediately practicable. The process, she knew well enough, would be a long and delicate one. Facts, she

148

was quite aware, must be faced and dealt with
one by one, and the most stubborn fact of all
—old Mrs. Millett, entrenched in her bedroom
with her formidable artillery of knocks—would
have to be overcome, or at least profoundly
modified before much progress could be made.
The one fact which at this time Aunt Janet
failed to take sufficiently into consideration was
little Miss Millett herself. It was not that she
had any idea of rescuing her in spite of herself :
there was nothing priggish or aggressive in
Aunt Janet's good deeds. The very notion of
compulsion would have seemed to her grotesque.
She held that every one should be free to develop
on his own lines, but that freedom, at least, was
essential ; and it was her idea of what actually
would be freedom for Miss Millett which led
her to leave *her*, as an obstacle, out of her
reckoning. And, after all, when the knight-
errant sets out to rescue the imprisoned maiden,
he does not expect to find that the maiden herself, as well as the dragon, is one of the obstacles
to his success.

Aunt Emily, of course, looked at the thing
from the opposite point of view. For *her*, Aunt
Janet's zeal for turning Miss Millett into something which could no longer, if names were to

be anything more than labels, be called Miss
Millett, was as absurd as to wish to turn Worcester
into Crown Derby. Miss Millett was what
circumstances had made her. To remove her
from her appropriate setting would be simply
to bewilder her and to spoil her particular charm.
Such an argument, if applied generally, results
simply in reaction and stagnation, but as applied
to Miss Millett and her peculiar circumstances
it contained a measure of truth which at that
time neither I nor Aunt Janet sufficiently recognized : it had even a certain delicacy and subtlety
which Aunt Janet's view lacked. For Aunt
Emily, Miss Millett was something exquisitely
fragile and beautiful, something to be loved
and protected ; but as for trying to change
her, it would be both an impertinence and a pro-
fanity.

" Suppose Miss Millett were to have the idea
of transforming you, Janet ! " she asked her
sister.

" My dear Emily," answered Aunt Janet :
" if you were to find a bird in a trap, would
you, or would you not, rescue it ? "

" Can you ask, Janet ? But it seems to me
to be a little barbarous to be so anxious to rescue
Miss Millett from the only surroundings in

which she is at home and from an invalid mother who is the very centre of her existence and who, besides, can ill spare her."

A few weeks later, an unexpected development occurred in the Millett affair. I had an account of the whole thing, shortly after it happened, from Aunt Janet's own lips. She had wired to me that she was coming up to town for the day and would be glad if I would lunch with her ; and no sooner were we seated at lunch than, needless to say, we fell upon the usual theme. Aunt Janet astounded me with the news that Miss Millett had spent the last month with them at Arleigh.

" How did I manage it ? " she laughed. " Why, I simply kipnapped her : at least that is what it amounted to. I had driven over to see her one morning and found her ill. Not in bed : the doctor had ordered her to bed, but her mother, she said, had forbidden it, and after all (she put it to me) if she did go to bed who would look after her mother ? At that, my dear, I lost my temper. I practically collared little Miss Millett (she was too ill to resist) ; I wrapped her up, bundled her into the carriage, and packed her off to Arleigh. Fortunately the

Milletts have a telephone, so I telephoned to Emily, explaining the state of affairs, and I also telephoned to Mrs. Millett's doctor to send a nurse to look after the old woman. Then I bearded her in her den. 'I am sorry to intrude, Mrs. Millett,' I said, 'but your daughter is so ill that she has been put to bed.' She was evidently astonished to see a stranger. A pair of eyes glared at me over the sheets. 'Put to bed?' she said. 'And by whom, pray?' 'By me,' I said; 'and I have also telephoned for a nurse to look after you.' 'Please ask Rose to come and speak to me at once,' said the old woman with determination. 'That, I am afraid, is impossible, Mrs. Millett,' said I, 'for she is in bed not here, but at my house some miles away. I was sure that it would be more convenient, as you yourself are an invalid, not to have another invalid in the house, so I just packed her off, out of the way, you see!' and I smiled ever so pleasantly at the old woman. 'She will be well cared for,' I went on; 'and until your nurse arrives I hope you will allow me to take her place. I shall be downstairs if you will knock, as usual.' But Mrs. Millett did not, apparently, like me and my ways. In the two hours during which I waited in the morning-room she did not knock once. Then the nurse arrived and I walked home.

"I found Rose in bed, of course, well looked after by Emily. She was really ill, poor little creature—so ill that she succumbed without a murmur to my somewhat highhanded tactics and simply gave herself up to the enjoyment of a complete rest in pleasant surroundings. I was careful, as you can imagine, to make the most of her illness. We kept her in bed for a fortnight and her doctor backed me up by assuring her that her mother was in the hands of a thoroughly competent nurse and would be all the better without her. After the fortnight Rose was allowed to get up. We stuffed her with good food and cheerful conversation and when she was well enough to go out we took her for drives. And you may be sure that I made the most of my opportunities, while we had her there, to undermine the tyranny of the old woman. I tried to get Rose to take up a definite attitude of her own towards her mother, instead of merely submitting to her. She had never, it seemed, realized the situation or examined her own feelings at all. It was rather like dealing with a child which had not yet become aware of itself. 'Tell me, Rose,' I

153

asked her one day, ' do you love your mother ? '
She looked at me with a funny little puzzled
look, as though I had given her a difficult sum
to do. ' I don't know,' she began hesitatingly.
' I've never really thought about it.' ' Are you
afraid of her ? ' She blushed and cast down
her eyes. ' Yes, I am, very much afraid of her.'
' But why should you be, my dear ? ' I said.
' After all, she can't do anything to you, can
she ? You should try to accustom her to the
thought that you are grown up and are determined to manage your own affairs. I don't
mean,' I said, ' that an invalid must not have
every consideration—every reasonable consideration ; but your mother, you know, my dear, is
fearfully tyrannical. If she had me to look
after her. . . .' But Rose did not allow me
to finish. The idea seemed to strike her
as tremendously amusing and she broke into
the first twitter of laughter I had heard from
her.

"However, I knew well enough that I could
not do much : I simply tried as well as I could
to feed up her mind and her self-reliance, just
as we were feeding up her frail little body. And
sure enough, as she became stronger, she began
to talk of returning home. ' Listen to me,

Rose,' I said to her. 'Do you really and truly want to return to your mother?' 'Yes,' she replied, avoiding my eye, 'really and truly.' 'You think that you will really feel happier at home? Now I want the truth, mind!' She gave me again that funny, puzzled look and was at first silent. 'Oh, not happier, certainly,' she began. 'But I feel I ought to go. Besides, Mamma has sent for me.' 'Sent for you, Rose?' 'Yes, I had a note from her this morning. Her nurse is not satisfactory.' 'You must allow me to answer that note, Rose,' I insisted; quite unwarrantably, I admit, but I was furious. And I answered it, somewhat in the style in which I had interviewed the old woman, saying that Rose was not well enough to write. But I knew, all along, that I was fighting a losing battle. That terrible moral compulsion which the old woman exercises on her was tightening its hold daily, and when I saw that it was destroying Rose's peace of mind, I confessed myself beaten. But at least she had had a good time—the happiest month of her life, she told us with a few irrepressible tears, poor dear. Her face, when she waved to us from the carriage window, still haunts me. It was the face of a child going to prison."

My next visit to Arleigh was several months later. The country was in the grip of a winter hard and bright as a diamond. Aunt Janet's flower-beds were hard and grey like cast-iron, so hard that one could walk on them without leaving a footprint : beneath one's heel they resounded hollow like the crust of a great pie. The lawn, too, was no longer the soft green expanse I had left last summer, but a grey, frost-cemented desert on which the busy black shapes of starlings and sparrows disputed the scraps which Aunt Janet scattered there. Sometimes a rook sailed down, tamed by the cold, stalked cautiously forward like an eccentric nonconformist parson and, sneaking the largest scrap, flew away with it, changing suddenly and miraculously as he left the ground, from awkwardness to soaring grace. The garden was still beautiful, though with a beauty not of Aunt Janet's making ; more pure, more magical than the beauty of summer and autumn. Every twig of every tree and shrub was furred with the minute crystals of the hoar-frost which had transformed the garden into an exquisite apparition of gleaming whiteness. I remember still how, gazing down each morning from my bedroom window into the misty sunlight, I seemed to be looking into a great crystal grotto in which every tree, invaded by a sudden luxuriance of scentless blossoms, stood fairylike over its steel-blue shadow. And the house, too, in that weather seemed even more beautiful than during the warm days. Its beauties appeared richer, the welcome of its warmth and colour more intimate than in the days when there was warmth and colour everywhere. Great log-fires crackled upon the hearths : the red glint of the flames flashed in the polished brass of fireplace, candlestick, and Flemish beaker, sparkled among the facets of old cut glass, or gleamed for a moment from the watery depths of a mirror or the glazed curve of a china vase. Soft carpets, deep chairs, and plump luxurious cushions invited one to a delicious laziness.

But in the neighbourhood of such a person as Aunt Janet there was no laziness during the daytime. Smart, bracing walks were the order of the day and it was not till tea-time that, responding to the invitation of those deep chairs and cushions, we grouped ourselves round the tea-table, while in the warm yellow lamplight Aunt Emily with serene face and white hands moving among the silver, faultlessly performed the ritual of pouring-out.

157

If I did not inquire at the moment of my arrival after Miss Millett, it was not from lack, but rather from excess of interest in her. That interest, I found, had been greatly increased by absence. It seemed, paradoxically, that in these last few months I had grown to be on much more familiar terms with her ; and when Aunt Janet greeted me on the platform on the afternoon of my arrival, it required a conscious effort to prevent myself from blurting out an inquiry almost before we had completed our greetings. And it was the same, I suspect, with Aunt Janet herself. The reason for her refraining from mentioning Rose throughout the whole of our drive from the station to the house was, I am sure, simply her consciousness of the extraordinary hold which Rose had taken of her. She doubtless felt that, to me who had so many other things to occupy me, she ran the risk of appearing crazed on the subject.

There were callers in the drawing-room when we arrived, and their presence seemed, somehow, to make it easier, for under cover of the general hum of conversation I found myself suddenly asking Aunt Janet about the Milletts. Aunt Janet went off like a mousetrap. " My dear," she said, seizing my arm, " that old woman is a perfect fiend."

That was all I could learn for the moment, but as soon as the callers had gone Aunt Janet settled down to report progress. The progress, alas! was all, since Rose had returned home, on the side of the old woman. She was obviously determined, once she had got Rose back into her clutches, that she should not escape again, and with the object, it seemed, of crushing all independence out of her, she now insisted on supervising everything she did. Rose now had to bring her a list of all the meals for the day —not only the old woman's meals, but of Rose's own and the servants'—and this she would rigorously correct. If Rose had written *boiled eggs*, the old woman cancelled it and wrote *poached eggs*: if Rose arranged for *stewed figs* they were at once altered to *stewed prunes*. The changes themselves were nothing, as poor Rose said to Aunt Janet, but it was just the fact that they were nothing that made the thing so infinitely more irritating and humiliating. The poor child was sometimes almost reduced to despair. Nor was that all. Each evening Rose had to render a detailed account of how she had spent the day, and if during the morning she appeared in a hat and coat, as though on the point of going out, the old woman would immediately determine that she could not spare her till the afternoon. "The thing," said Aunt Janet, "would be ludicrous if it were not so terrible. On a merely physical basis, the old woman is so absolutely helpless that if Rose were to refuse to obey any of those rules, they would simply collapse. Rose herself knows it, but the old woman possesses such a complete control of her mind that she can do what she likes with her. And the worst of it is that *we* can do almost nothing. The most I can do now is to take Rose for walks. The old woman doesn't know, of course, or she would stop it at once. Rose and I agree on a day and an hour and I wait for her down the road about a hundred yards from their gate. We have had one or two jolly walks together, and those walks mean a great deal to Rose : at least I have the satisfaction of knowing that. We are having a walk to-morrow, and you must come too."

Next day the frost still held and the hard brilliance of winter sunshine filled heaven and earth. After a smart cross-country tramp, Aunt Janet and I arrived punctually at the appointed place and (for a wonder, said Aunt Janet) we were the first on the spot. In fact Rose was late. We waited for a quarter of an hour and still she did not come. For another quarter of an hour we paced up and down the road and then we turned into a gap in the hedge and sat on a gate in the sunshine. " She will have to pass us," said Aunt Janet, " on her way to the meeting-place."

We had not been there long before we heard a sound of running on the road, and we climbed down from our gate. Then, as the running approached us, the sound of a fall. Then renewed running, but slower now, and as we emerged on to the road we came upon Rose white-faced, exhausted, struggling for breath with dry sobs. Her hands were bleeding and she had torn a hole in her skirt at the knee, and when Aunt Janet hurried up to her she dissolved into such an agonized fit of weeping that at first she could not speak. As if comforting a child, Aunt Janet soothed her in her warm, motherly way and examined the scratched hands. " Oh, it's not that," sobbed Rose, looking at her hands : " but I thought you had gone. I thought I had missed you. She wouldn't let me come." Her sobs broke out again. How pathetic, how forlorn she looked at that moment in her despair ! The memory of it still wakes a flood of pity in me and the same feeling of helplessness and frustration which I then felt, because I could do nothing to help and comfort her. I walked ahead while Aunt Janet soothed her and bathed her hands with snow.

It was really her own fault, she explained to Aunt Janet, because, just when she was starting to meet us, her mother had knocked and she had answered the knock in her hat and coat. The result, of course, was that the old woman insisted on being read to. Rose begged to be allowed to go, but the result of that was that the reading protracted itself till Rose, torn between fear of her mother and despair at missing Aunt Janet, had rushed from the room and out of the house. It sounds, perhaps, a small and insignificant matter now, as I tell it, but to us who saw it and knew little Miss Millett and all the cruel circumstances of her life, that frantic escape from home, the fall, the sudden fit of weeping, and afterwards the brief tremulous delight which she took in her walk with us, a delight that seemed out of all proportion to so small an event—all these things typified and focused into one point the tragedy of her thwarted and starved life.

And then suddenly, within a month, old Mrs.
162

Millett died. Aunt Janet, when next I met her in town, was exultant. The thought that the hateful grip had suddenly fallen from Rose had lifted a load from her mind. Not that she ignored the fact that Mrs. Millett's death and the complete transformation of her own life would be a severe shock for Rose : but that would be merely temporary, and soon she would enjoy a freedom and health which she had never before dreamed of.

Aunt Janet, then, showed no indecent haste : it was she knew, a question of time. All that remained for her to do was to help Rose to some confidence in herself, to advise, direct, sometimes perhaps to bring a little wise pressure to bear when Rose, from force of habit, showed signs of ignoring the possibilities of freedom.

The day after the funeral, when the various relatives who always materialize on such occasions had disappeared, Aunt Janet walked over to see Rose, and, as it turned out, she was the very thing that Rose was longing for. "I found her," Aunt Janet told me, "actually watching for me at the window, and before I could ring the bell she had opened the door. It was a different Rose, an even less apprehensible one than before, so strange, so transformed she was with her black dress and her white, scared little face. The incongruous black dress, so far from bringing her to earth, made her by contrast the more elusive, the more fairylike. The fairy, with its beseeching blue eyes and the golden haze of its hair, looked plaintively out of its absurd disguise, afraid, it seemed, of being laughed at, thus lamentably ensnared in a fashion and pining for its pools and leaves. She ran forward, seized my arm, and drew me in. ' I knew you would come,' she said. ' I have been watching for you. I wanted to walk and meet you, but I felt I ought not perhaps to go out yet.' She took me into the morning-room and we sat talking in low voices. There was a constraint upon us—that feeling, usual at such times, that it was somehow wrong to talk freely and naturally, and that our talk and attitude must conform to some undefined convention. And the black dress, too, was a barrier between us. Not only did it make Rose different for me ; it obviously made her different for herself. But it was not only that. The house was empty, unbelievably empty. That old woman who had never moved from her bedroom for years had so pervaded it that it had become, even for me, a materialization of her personality ; and now

164

that she was dead, the house too seemed dead and cast a chill upon us. Footsteps moved in the room above : no doubt it was being cleaned and all the medical apparatus which accumulates about an invalid removed. Those sounds, I could see, embarrassed Rose and she seemed to be unable to refer to them. I began to say that I hoped she would soon walk over to see us and that I hoped, too, that we should do many walks together. Then a dreadful thing happened. Two sharp knocks rapped upon the ceiling. Rose, with the same terrified little 'Oh,' sprang to her feet and I jumped as I always used to jump. 'Oh !' said Rose with a timid smile. 'What a fright I got ! I thought . . . I thought . . .' and there she stopped, feeling perhaps that she was speaking her unconscious thought too plainly. It was as though the old woman were reminding us that, although her body was gone, we still had her to reckon with, and soon I found that we were talking in whispers and that I was avoiding the remotest reference to Rose's freedom. With an effort I spoke louder. Rose flinched. Then by a happy thought I inquired after the garden. The effect was immediate. Rose smiled : we opened the French window and went out. Out-of-doors, it seemed that a load had been lifted from us. We spoke in our accustomed tones without difficulty. Rose moved intently from plant to plant, asking questions about pruning and taking cuttings, proudly pointing out the luxuriance of her lavender hedge. In a week she would be busy gathering the lavender. It would take her a whole day, at least : then it would have to be dried in the sun and stripped, and she had the wonderful idea of trying to make lavender water. So she chattered, thoughtless, happy as a singing bird, oblivious, now, of her black dress. Then, as she stretched out her hand to gather a rose for me, I saw her catch sight of her sleeve. The look of constraint came back into her face and I felt that she was on the point of glancing shyly up at me to see if I too had remembered. But when she did look up, I was gazing at the rose and she, thinking that the little incident had passed unnoticed, relapsed into her happy mood again.

"We lingered till dusk about her garden or pacing up and down the lawn, till the evening damp had chilled us to the bone. Both of us were fighting against the necessity of going back into the house and we never, in our perambulations, turned the corner of the house into the

166

hard, brilliant garden before the front-door. So we paced, preferring weariness and cold to the oppression of the house and I postponing my departure in my reluctance to leave Rose alone with the watchful presence of the departed Mrs. Millett. For that, to be honest, was what I felt was pervading the house. It was not, I felt now, an emptiness that the old woman's departure had left nor the hush which death leaves for a while behind it : it was, for me at least, the feeling that she herself was there in a subtler, more pervading, more malevolent form than when she had lain upstairs in her bedroom. And it occurred to me, inexplicably, that if I were now to go into her bedroom I should feel that room to be the only one in the house where she was *not*. I tried to persuade Rose to return with me to Arleigh for some days, but she would not. She said simply that she ought not to go away so soon, and if she had added, as her reason, ' Mamma might be angry ! ' I should hardly, I believe, have been surprised. When I finally left her it was quite dark, and, looking back as I closed the gate, I saw her still in the porch, small and lonely, under the mournful light of the hideous gas-lamp. And suddenly the absurd but quite inescapable feeling overcame me that I was leaving her a prey to a sinister, inapprehensible influence which was now in possession of the house."

Both Aunt Janet and Aunt Emily were agreed, though as usual for opposite reasons, that Rose ought to leave her home. She should leave, according to Aunt Emily, because by leaving a place with so many associations she would more easily become reconciled to her loss. " The most sensible thing," she said, " is to be ruthless on such occasions and simply to cut oneself off from the old life." Aunt Janet agreed that Rose should " cut herself off," but for the reason that to do so would be to escape from slavery. " To be more exact," she said to me, " Rose must cut herself off from the old woman and all that represents her : and that house, my dear, as I have told you before, is simply full of Mrs. Millett."

But when these schemes were in course of time gently broached to Rose, she was not, to the astonishment of Aunt Janet, in the least disposed to fall in with them. " I feel that I really ought not to leave the house," she said, and that, for some time, was all that they could

get out of her. Aunt Janet tried gentle argument. " There is no *ought* about it, my dear.
You are free to do exactly as you feel inclined."

" Yes, yes, I know," replied Rose timidly :
" but I really feel I couldn't."

" You *couldn't*, Rose ? "

" No, if I went anywhere else I should . . ."
she hesitated, and then added shamefacedly,
" well, I should feel lost."

" Till then," Aunt Janet told me, " I had
not completely realized Rose's attitude towards
the outside world. She regards it, John . . .
well, much as you and I regard the interior of
Persia. She is really afraid of uprooting herself
from the one little patch of the world that she
knows. She has, you see, lived the life of a
nun."

And so, for the time, the subject was dropped,
and for weeks after that Rose lived on at the
house as usual, working in her small garden,
tiptoeing about the house as she had done when
her mother was alive, taking out and replacing
the books in her bottom shelf. Once, when
Aunt Janet suggested that she should dismiss
two rows of bound magazines from the upper
shelves in the morning-room to the boxroom
and extend her own library, she answered with

a timid, bewildered and slightly reproachful look which seemed to say, "Please don't make me try to reason about it. Leave me to do as I feel." And so she continued, living as it were on sufferance, in obedience to some strange compulsion, in what was now her own house. "In fact," said Aunt Janet, "the child is still under the thumb of the old woman."

My next news, however, showed a triumph for the Aunts. Rose was going abroad with them. They were starting almost immediately and would be away for several months. It was to be Italy and Switzerland. "When we have crossed the Channel," Aunt Janet wrote to me, "I shall feel at last that Rose is liberated." And I too felt, when I had a post-card from them in Paris, that the problem of Rose, which had absorbed us both for so long, was solved at last.

But a letter from Florence a month later gave the impression that the problem was not, after all, completely solved. "Rose," it ran, "is undoubtedly better and she is undoubtedly enjoying herself, but her mind is in a curious condition. In her normal state she is cheerful and keenly interested in everything about her.

She spends hours in churches and galleries with
Emily, studying Giotto, Fra Angelico, Botticelli,
and the rest of them, and she is never tired of
wandering in the streets with me and taking
long walks into the country beyond Fiesole and
Settignano. But she is subject to sudden moods.
Once or twice, when looking at pictures with
Emily, once when exploring the Borgo degli
Albizzi with me, she suddenly declared that she
must return immediately to the hotel. Her only
reason was that it was half-past twelve (or whatever time it happened to be) and that she *must*.
One day when I pressed her to explain, she
laid her hand on my arm : ' Please don't ask
me why,' she said. ' It's simply that I *must* ' ;
and that was all I could get out of her—all, I
am persuaded, that she herself knew. Last
Thursday, for the first time, something more
startling occurred. We were sitting together in
the Boboli Gardens and had been silent for
some minutes when I noticed something unusual
about Rose. She had fallen, it seemed, into a
sort of waking dream. She sat with her body
bent forward, oblivious of her surroundings, and
stared before her with a wide, empty intensity.
Her expression alarmed me and I watched her
quietly, thinking it better not to rouse her. She

remained in that state for a quarter of an hour. Then, suddenly exclaiming, ' All right, I'm coming ! ' she jumped from her chair, hurried away for a few yards, and then apparently awoke. She seemed quite scared and ashamed—poor child—at what she had done. Such symptoms, as you can imagine, are very disquieting, the more so to me who know all the circumstances, for I get the horrible feeling—absurd, of course, I know—that the old woman is still trying to get hold of her. And, after all, John, it is not so absurd in a sense, because the old woman is undoubtedly responsible for these strange fits. How much, I only discovered yesterday when something of the same sort happened again. We were sitting in the lounge, she and I, when a man who had been writing letters at the other end of the room, knocked over a chair as he went out. I myself jumped a little, but poor Rose, who was sitting beside me reading, sprang to her feet and with a white, terrified face ran towards the door. Then she recollected herself and came back, all confused, to her seat beside me and wept a little, poor child, before she could settle down to her reading again. That occurrence reminded me of Mrs. Millett's knocks, and as I sat afterwards thinking things over, it suddenly struck me that Rose's strange impulses to hurry home at certain moments always come to her at or after 12.30, 4 o'clock, or 6.30, the hours at which she used to carry up her mother's meals. It is, you see, as though under some inescapable compulsion she were unconsciously repeating the old routine."

Several weeks later, Aunt Janet writes from Verona. "It is getting too hot for us here. In a week or so we shall probably move on for Switzerland. Rose is much the same : well and cheerful for the most part, but with the same strange fits of abstraction. I had hoped that they would decrease with time, but they have certainly not done so since last I wrote : in fact, they are, I'm afraid, a little more frequent. Strange child ! she asked me, the other day, if I could remember the address of Robson the nursery-gardener, and it turned out that she was writing to arrange for . . . what do you think ? . . . the bedding-out in front of the house. Yes, it *must* be done, she says, exactly the same as usual ; and I seemed to feel, in the silence that followed, ' Mamma will be so angry if it isn't.' "

Towards the end of August Aunt Janet writes from Montana. " Rose is ill and I am alarmed about her. The doctor cannot say yet whether it is sunstroke or some affection of the brain. At times she is delirious and talks and talks, endlessly repeating oh, such dreadful, such heartrending things. I am haunted by the feeling that the influence of that terrible old woman is gradually enclosing her. You will think, John, that your Aunt Janet is going crazy, and, as a matter of fact, I am, I think, somewhat overwrought from nursing her."

A letter a few days later startled me. Not that its news was more alarming than the last, but when letters come frequently in times of illness, one feels half consciously, you know, that things are worse. " Rose is no better," it ran, " but, I think, no worse. This afternoon she had a good sleep and seemed the better for it. Afterwards, we talked quietly and happily for an hour. She keeps referring to her garden —her own little garden, I mean—and is anxious about her lavender. The crop will be spoiled if it is not cut soon. John, will you think it foolish of me if I ask you to go and cut it for her and send it out here ? "

Next morning I left town with an empty suit-case to gather Rose's lavender. The day was still misty when I left the train and started

174

on the two-mile walk to the Milletts' house. It was misty, and although it was only August, there was an autumnal sting and a sweetness of premature decay in the air. I had not been near the house since that brilliant, frosty day when Aunt Janet and I had waited for Rose on the road. Now the obscuring impressions of all the events which had happened since then, the persistent thought of Rose's illness, and perhaps the fact that I was alone, gave me the sensation of being somehow displaced from reality—of moving in an unreal but poignant vision in which my senses worked with a strange sharpness, but the feelings I derived from them were numbed and altered from their usual current. As I opened the gate, the house stared at me sightlessly with bolted doors and drawn blinds, but the garish spectacle of blazing flower-beds and close-shaven grass greeted me as before, as if the harsh spirit of old Mrs. Millett still held the place in its power ; and for a moment I half wondered if I should find that those fierce geraniums, calceolarias, and lobelias had spread to Rose's garden too and choked its delicate and fragrant beauty. But when I rounded the corner of the house, I found that a different power had been at work there—the slow, encroaching power

of Nature. For Rose's garden had been neg-
lected and her flowers bloomed among a thicket
of weeds and tall-flowering grasses about which
the lavender hedge, grown thick and high since
I had laſt seen it on the day when Aunt Janet
and I firſt went to tea there, raised its shock of
grey-green ſtalks and pale violet heads. And as
I ſtood looking at it now and remembering
what it had been when Rose herself showed it
to us, it seemed to me that years and years had
passed in the meantime and that I was already
an old man full of old memories and old sorrows.

It took me half a day to reap Rose's lavender-
harveſt and it was late afternoon when I packed
the bundles into my suit-case, dropped in among
them a ſtolen bunch of the little roses which
ſtill bloomed there, and left the shorn hedge
surrounding its dense little thicket. I rounded
Mrs. Millett's blazing parterres and let the iron-
spiked gate swing-to behind me. Then, obey-
ing a sudden impulse—sentimental, if you like,
but quite genuine—I walked, before setting off
for the ſtation, a few yards up the road and
ſtood again at the spot where Rose had fallen
and wept so bitterly the very laſt time I had
seen her. . . .

When I got home that evening. another letter

lay on my table and, as I recognized Aunt
Janet's handwriting, I felt my heart suddenly
contract, and I paused before opening the
envelope and suddenly lost consciousness of my
surroundings in a profound reverie. I was
young then and I had never, I believe, up till
that moment analysed my feelings towards Rose.
She was such a strange little thing, charming
but so elusive—physically so childlike, so fairy-
like—that the idea of falling in love with her
had never entered my head. But my life, like
Aunt Janet's, had become more and more absorbed into hers, and though I was, even now,
not yet, I think, consciously in love with her, I
was in a state very near to it, for I discovered
all at once that I had been looking forward to
her return with a sort of subdued excitement,
and that for some weeks all my visions of the
future had been focused into our meeting again.
But at the sight of Aunt Janet's handwriting on
the letter, my future had suddenly withered,
crumbled, dissolved into dust. I knew already
what the letter had to tell me. "Do not trouble,"
it ran, "if you have not already done so, about
the lavender. Our dear Rose died last night.
To you, who know how I feel, I need say no
more. Perhaps if we had known her six or

seven years earlier. . . . However, why should we imagine things which have not happened? As it is, we were too late. I realized it finally and completely in her laſt words to me. She was unconscious for some time before she died, but juſt before the end she opened her eyes and looked up at me, a little surprised, with that clear, innocent look of hers. ' Promise me one thing,' she said. I promised. ' That you will bury me beside Mamma.' "

Calder had finished. The ſtory had taken so long that it was already supper-time, and he insiſted on my having supper with him before I set off for home. He drew a bottle of '68, and as we drank it the memory of poor Rose quietly dissolved as I had seen the lavender-smoke dissolve earlier in the afternoon.

Mrs. Lovelace

I

WHEN THE MASTER OF THE house dies, the blinds are drawn, and the house is closed in upon itself, its life governed by the unforgettable presence in the room upstairs. But after the dead man has been carried downstairs and borne to his grave, the house opens its eyes again upon the world and little by little renews its ordered rhythm. Such a thing had befallen me. I had crouched, dumb and blind, like a darkened house before the one absorbing fact of my disaster. And when at last I began to look outwards again I felt that new scenes and bodily exercise were necessary to enable me to regain possession of myself. Then, as I groped rather faint-heartedly for a plan, I remembered that six-days' walk I had taken ten years ago—fifty years ago it seemed now—through the valleys and among the hills of that remote countryside when autumn was slowly and gorgeously burning itself out. That autumnal countryside had remained in my memory as a sanctuary to which my mind could return again and again for refreshment ; and as in the course of time the actual details had faded, the sensation of the place had become intensified, till now it returned to me more as a rich melody than as an assemblage of tangible facts. Then, as my mind was submerged once more in that mellow atmosphere—that old, inevitable, never-ending tune—it penetrated to the heart of the thing, the person who had been for me the meaning, the reality, of which all those enchanting things were only the symbols, and like the return of swallows in the spring, detail after detail came back into my memory, building up again the whole experience.

It was during the last days of my holiday that I had met Mrs. Lovelace. In a morning sharp with dew and bright with sunshine, I had climbed to a great undulating heath, a rolling sea of copper-coloured bracken that spread like a double tide to either margin of the moorland road and foamed about the feet of sombre firs which dotted the heath with rare islands. From there at noon the road dropped towards the valley again ; trees crowded up to its edges and stood there, many-shaped and many-coloured, in hanging cascades of crimson and orange, sudden puffs of scarlet fire, or upward-leaping fountains of blond foam. At the bottom of the valley the road skirted a small tree-girdled lake, round and deep like a great inverted dome, in whose concavity the burning colours of the trees were blurred and melted in the dark transparency of the water. And long after the lake had passed behind me, I had come upon that lonely inn by the roadside and knew from my map that I was now eight miles from the village where I had planned to pass the night. Then, as I continued on my way, I began to regret my swift passage, and to think that I should do better to stay the night at the inn I had just passed and so linger a little among those surroundings. Just as I had resolved to do so, I came upon her round a bend of the road. At first the freedom and alertness of her step made me think she was a girl, and even when we came face to face her bright complexion and clear eyes would have confirmed the belief had it not been for her white hair and something calm and mature in her expression which was beautiful beyond the beauty of youth. As an excuse to speak to her, I stopped and asked her about the inn, and when she told me that she lived there it was one reason the more that I should break my journey there.

And a delightful inn it was—a little tumbledown place, yet everything about it was charming : the landlord with his humorous, weather-beaten face ; the landlady shy, dark-haired, and quietly attentive to one's well-being ; and their child Mary, a lovely little girl of eight, half flower, half confiding little animal. But the most noticeable thing about them was their affection for Mrs. Lovelace. It was she, one felt, who was the mainspring of the whole affair. It was somehow because of her that the landlord was so friendly and so comical, the landlady so anxious that you should be happy, and the child such a lovable little creature. Yes, evidently Mrs. Lovelace had enchanted the place. When she came into the room, one felt an access of well-being ; when she left it, it was as though some one had blown out a light. And she was always entering and leaving the room, busy, it seemed, about lending a hand with the house-work. Sometimes she would flit in and up to a cupboard carrying plates and glasses, or pass —a sudden apparition—from one door to another leading a dog, or her light footstep would cross the ceiling, her clear voice call from the garden at the back of the house. And whenever one saw her or heard her, one felt a glow of satis-faction. There was no resisting, and I too was drawn into the scheme—became yet another satellite revolving round that central radiance ; and I lingered there for days, unwilling to exile myself from such a delicious state of things. One laughed and talked and enjoyed one's food, or told fairy-stories to the little girl—all because of Mrs. Lovelace : and none of the stories told was more enchantingly impossible than the actual life that we led there.

On the day of my departure an old parson turned up for lunch ; he had walked over from his vicarage four miles away. He was received as an old friend, it was almost as if they were expecting him, and we all sat down together to a jovial lunch. My road to the station lay through his village, and when I set off on my eight miles' walk he went with me.

" Well," he said, after we had finished our good-byes and were getting into our stride, " I hope you have fallen in love with Mrs. Lovelace ? "

" Certainly I have," I replied.

" That's right," he said. " Everybody does."

" I can hardly imagine the place existing without her," I went on. " The inn, the landlord, his wife, and that delightful little child, the whole delicious life of the place seem to

me . . . well, simply reflections, manifestations
of Mrs. Lovelace."

"And yet," said the parson, "there was a
time—nearly half a century ago, it is true—
before she came. I knew her as a child of six,
and twelve years later I remember her coming
to the inn, a mere girl still, with her husband.
She had bolted with him, God bless her. Her
people had refused their consent : he had no
money—she hadn't much : two hundred a year,
I believe—and he was considered to be beneath
her in station. So he was. But he was as fine
a young fellow as you could wish to meet : in
the Mercantile Marine : he had signed on with
a ship in the China trade which was off in a
few weeks time on a five years' voyage, and
her people insisted—hoping, of course, that the
affair would blow over altogether—that they
should at least wait till he returned. I didn't
sympathize with their views. The two young
people were head over ears in love, and, as I
said, he was a first-rate chap, one in ten thousand.
So I was delighted, despite my cloth, when I
heard one afternoon that she had packed up and
bolted with him. They came to the inn for
their honeymoon, and when the time came for
him to go she stayed on there during the five

years of his absence, cheerfully awaiting his return. And at last he was back again—back for a couple of months. You met them together all over the country doing day-long rambles together. Their perfect happiness was visible to all. Every one knew them and looked out for them, deriving a sort of reflected happiness from the sight of them. Then he went away again, but this time he never came back. It was fever he died of, I believe, somewhere in the China Sea. I was afraid it would be the end of her ; but I was wrong, absurdly wrong, for after the first shock she rallied and soon recovered herself completely. It seemed—how can I express it ?—as if their happiness in one another had not been destroyed by his death, but rather that it remained with her, not as a mere memory, a consolation to be found only by introspective brooding, but as a living reality. You remember the words of Christ : ' I am the water of life : he that drinketh of Me shall never thirst.' So it is with Mrs. Lovelace : she tasted once of perfect happiness and, as you see, she still has enough not only for herself but also for the whole countryside. I turn up, as I turned up to-day, once a month, to renew my supply."

We parted, the old parson and I, when we reached his village.

"Good-bye, good-bye," he said. "And don't forget to go back to the inn when your supply runs short." He stood with one hand on his gate, and, waving the other to me, vanished out of my life. . . .

II

Like a diver curving up from his cool rush through dim water into a dazzle of sunlight, I came up out of my dip into the past and awoke to the desolation of my unhappy present. The old boy's words were still in my mind. Certainly now, if ever, my supply had run short. What could be better, then, than to go back to the inn and Mrs. Lovelace ? I looked out trains and packed my knapsack.

When, having reached my destination, I left the slow little train to draw its plume of smoke among the harvests of the valley and made my way uphill into the heart of the country, I felt that I had stepped straight back into that life into which I had dipped for a few days ten years ago. Yet it was not exactly the same, because everything about me exhaled that poignant and baffling intensity, that more-than-reality, with

which scenes revisited after a long interval sometimes assail the senses. The still fires and
standing fountains of autumn filled the country,
as before, with a transforming splendour ; un-
moving, everlasting, it would have seemed under
the still autumn sunshine, if here and there a
red leaf floating vertically to the ground had not
portended the beginning of change. The days
were cloudless as ten years ago, and when I
reached the small, dark lake it was incredibly,
piercingly the same. I could almost have believed
that the colours of those blurred and mingled
reflections had never faded from its round deep
mirror but had smouldered on for ten years as
they had smouldered, half-forgotten but unextin-
guished, in my mind. And all the time I kept
expecting to meet Mrs. Lovelace : at every turn
in the road, at every opening in the trees, I
kept wondering that she did not appear. I
remembered the old parson's story. " You met
them," he had said, " all over the country, doing
long rambles together." And that country
lived in my memory so entirely as part of the
mind of Mrs. Lovelace, that it seemed irrational
that the old scenes should reappear and yet she
be absent.

When I reached the inn the sun had already

gone down, but it was hardly dusk enough to draw the blinds, so that to find the inn with its blinds drawn and its windows dark came to me as a shock. But as I rounded the house I saw an upstairs window—hers, I was sure—brightly illuminated, with the blind still undrawn, and at once I felt reassured ; it was so typical of her and her relation to the inn. Yet it was strange and not so typical, I reflected, that the light should all be concentrated into one room and the rest of the place should be dark. And when I entered it was stranger still, for there was dimness and silence. It was as though some one had blown out a candle. At the sound of my feet the landlady appeared. Her face chilled me to the bone. It was not that she received me coldly : though she did not at first recognize me—and how should she, so changed as I was ?—her greeting had the same quiet kindness. But I missed something in her face, and again the phrase came to me " as though some one had blown out a candle." In a voice I could hardly control, I asked after Mrs. Lovelace.

" She's gone," she replied.

" Gone ? " I said. " Left you for good ? " She nodded.

"Surely you did not quarrel?"

"How could we quarrel?" she answered with a quivering smile. She said no more, and I dared not question her further.

"And the child?" I asked. At that a light flickered for a moment in her eyes.

"Mary was married yesterday," she answered. The door opened, and the landlord came in and we sat, all three, in the twilight, talking over the fire. In him too I felt that withdrawal of the former flame which I had felt from the moment of my arrival both in the landlady and in the whole atmosphere of the inn. His old humour was numbed and muted, a ghost of its former joviality. Again and again the name of Mrs. Lovelace rose to my lips, and always something in myself, something in them, deprived me of courage to speak of her. Even when the landlady went upstairs to prepare my room, the landlord and I talked only of other things.

When she returned, I went up to wash and take off my dusty boots.

"The same room as last time," she told me, with a faint smile. "The second on the left."

I climbed the stairs. A floor-board at the stair-head wheezed beneath my foot—a sharp, familiar reminder of my former visit, but in the

semi-darkness of the passage my memory failed
me for a moment, and when at laſt I opened
the door which I thought was mine, a surprising
vision confronted me, for the room was brightly
illuminated and full of a rich scent. Candles
shone on the mantelpiece and in the mirror
behind them their refleĉtions answered them
with a milder and more miſty glow. There
were more candles on the table, and as my eyes
grew accuſtomed to the soft brightness, I saw
in a corner of the room an arbour of autumnal
boughs, scarlet, orange, and crimson, built like
a canopy above the bed. Then with a shock I
saw beneath the carefully-spread white counter-
pane the mould of a human body. My eyes
ran up to the pillow, but on the pillow I could
see nothing but a cluſter of large white lilies.
There was a soft footfall behind me. It was
the landlady with a candle in her hand. She
closed the door and came up to me. " Come
and look," she whispered, and with her I approached the bed on tiptoe and found between
the lilies what I had expeĉted to find—the face
of Mrs. Lovelace. The pallor of death had not
diminished its beauty, indeed it had added a
touch of frail youthfulness which was not there
before. The thick hair drawn back from her

temples shone in the yellow candlelight not white but the fairest flaxen. It was as though she had become a girl again. And so happy, so serene was her expression that it was impossible, as we stood looking at her, to feel otherwise than happy and serene.

"Those lilies," said the landlady, "are what Mary carried at her wedding." She attended to the candles and smoothed the edge of the pillow as though for a sleeper, and we went out together.

"Come down into the kitchen," she said, "and I'll tell you all that happened.

"Two years ago," she began, when I was seated between her and her husband before the fire, "when Mary was eighteen, she and a young fellow near here began courting. He was such a good boy in every way that we were glad, in spite of the fact that he was so poor that, even with what we could give Mary, there was no hope that they would be able to wed for years. Two years went by and they were fonder than ever of each other, but he was as far as ever, seemingly, from earning anywhere near enough to keep a wife. Then, one day not long ago, he came along to say that he was going to Australia. A cousin of his father's had offered him a place there and it seemed the only chance of getting a paying job.

"Mary did her best to take it reasonable-like, but you could see how hard it hit her. At the end of the week the poor child was as pinched and pale as if she had been at death's door. It was then that our dear Mrs. Lovelace stepped in. She had only waited, seemingly, to make quite sure of them, and now she simply said that Mary's boy was not to go to Australia but stay at home and get married at once, because she was going to give them her own money. 'You know my story,' she said, 'well, the best part of that is going to happen over again.' That was a month ago. It was arranged that the two should be wedded yesterday. But a fortnight ago Mrs. Lovelace was taken bad. We never dreamt it was serious till she got worse and we sent for the doctor. She knew she was dying, but the idea of that didn't trouble her at all, and she remained her old self almost to the end. 'Don't worry,' she said. 'I shan't die till after they're married,' and she wouldn't let us change the arrangements.

"Yesterday—the day of the wedding, that is —I sat with her while they all went to the church, and when it was over my man came up and gave us an account of it, and she listened to it all, as pleased and interested as could be. Then in the evening the two young ones came and sat with her. She knew them, though she was almost past speaking by that time, but when they said good night to her she whispered something to Mary. 'It's for you now, Mary,' she said, 'to keep the inn going.' Now what could she mean by that, do you think? Nothing, most likely, for I reckon her poor mind was wandering. Soon after the young ones left her she fell asleep and slept on without a break till, just after midnight, as I was sitting by her bed, I heard a little catch in her breath. I turned, but her breathing had begun again, only more softly now. Then, twenty minutes later, there was another little catch and after that the breathing did not recommence."

The dusk had deepened during the landlady's story and when she finished we sat in darkness. Then there came a sound of wheels on the road. "It's Mary," said the landlady, and she rose eagerly and lighted the lamp : but it was the change in their faces that amazed me more than the growing light of the lamp, for all that I had missed there till then flowed visibly back like the lighting of many candles. There was a step, a click of the latch, and Mary stood in the doorway like an apparition, with the gold of her hair shining in the lamplight. And suddenly, not because of any bodily resemblance, but in some subtle, inexplicable, spiritual way, I seemed to be again in the magical presence of Mrs. Lovelace.

The Inn

LONG AND LOW LIKE A BARN, THE inn stood by the roadside at the highest point of the pass. At its southern end, intersected by cinder-paths, a small garden had been carved out of the bare hillside, where sparse vegetables sprouted and a few forlorn damson-trees leaned away from the prevailing wind. Before and behind the inn gaunt screes rose bare against the sky : in fine weather their blackness was starred with the dazzling sparkle of quartz ; when it rained they shone coldly like silver, and in time of storm the clatter of their sliding shale was heard at intervals above the shuddering of the wind and the long hiss of driven rain. The landlord could rely on a fair turnover in liquor because the pass was the only means of communication between the villages in the valleys on either side of it, and the ascent to it was thirsty work. In earlier days it had been the favourite resort of the rowdier members of the nearer villages or of those who, for reasons of their own, preferred to avoid the society of the village authorities. But in recent years a new landlord had taken it over, the place had been restored, and a new-fashioned bar put in ; and either through a change of preference in its former disreputable patrons or a lack of cordiality to them in the new landlord, it had now become a thoroughly respectable public-house.

On an afternoon in these its regenerate days two travellers had approached the inn from opposite directions and now sat drinking their beer and chatting to the host in the clean bar-parlour. One was a farmer, a short burly fellow in breeches and gaiters, with powerful shoulders, big hands, big knees. The other was dry, thin, and spectacled, his dryness redeemed by a well-shaped and humorous mouth. He was a school-master who spent his holidays in exploring the country. They talked of inns and compared the inns of their youth with the inns of their middle-age.

" Ah, yes," said the farmer, by way of supplying a bridge to the conversation which had suddenly flagged, as conversations among strangers sometimes will. " Ah, yes, I've known some queer inns in my time. And so have you, I expect, sir," he nodded at the schoolmaster.

" I have," said the schoolmaster with an odd movement at the corners of his mouth.

" I remember one," the farmer continued, " Oh, many years ago now—a lonely place it was, and very much the worse for wear—that I used to look into from time to time, just for a half-pint. The occasion I am thinking of was a blustery evening in autumn. It was already dark. I had had a long tramp and I had a long tramp still in front of me, and I felt that a drink would help matters a bit. So when I came abreast of the inn and saw a light under the door and heard the sound of a fiddle inside, I had a mind to go in. But when I had opened the door I didn't go in at once. I stood there for a moment dazed. It wasn't so much the light that dazed me : it was the sudden change from the quiet dark behind me to the racket and confusion that faced me. Opening that door, gentlemen, was like letting an angry dog loose on yourself. What with the shouting and chattering of the crowd, the hot stench of wood-smoke and tobacco-smoke and beer, the squeaking and scratching of the fiddle, and the lights and shadows going round and round like great shadowy whip-tops . . . it was hell let loose and no mistake. ' Well,' says I to myself, ' here goes ! ' and I put my head down and took a dive into the pandemonium.

"Most of them were a rum lot : a tramp or two, a gipsy or two, and a few young farm-

hands from the neighbouring villages, and I
caught sight of young Tom among them, the
landlord's son, a good-for-nothing young lout
who had been cashiered from the army nine
months before and, ever since, had been drinking
himself to death at home. Then as I began to
see through the smoke and dazzle and the
dancing, I saw they'd got a girl or two with
them as well. Well, the fiddle music jerked on
and on, and the feet on the stone floor went
on grinding and grinding, till it seemed as if
the whole thing was hitched on to a threshing-
machine. But at last the fiddler stopped and
the dance fell to pieces. Then with a screeching
of chairs and a banging of mugs on the table
and a gabbling and a giggling, the dancers got
sat down, and I saw that the music had come
from Long Jonathan, who sat quietly in the
corner with a mug of beer at his elbow. I
knew the country round about there pretty well,
and so I knew Long Jonathan. Jonathan was
one of the institutions, so to speak. I fancy he
must have been a sailor once, because he wore
gold ear-rings. Time out of mind he had walked
that country playing the fiddle, and every one
was glad to see him, not only because he was
a first-class fiddler, but also because he was an

honeſt chap with a lot of good ſtories, and as comical as you like, though you wouldn't have thought it at firſt, he was so quiet. And he was sharp with his tongue too, was Jonathan : a wonderful fellow at repartee. I remember one night, young Tom (before he was cashiered, this was !) called Jonathan ' Old Scratchguts.' ' What's the use,' says Tom ' of tramping the country wearing out catgut all your life ? '— ' Not much use that I knows of,' answers Jonathan, ' but more, perhaps, than wearing out your own guts with whisky.' Not bad, that ! " and the farmer gave a roar and brought a huge hand down on a huge knee.

" Well, everybody had more drink and there was a great roar of talking and laughing and clouds of baccy smoke and the giggling and squealing of the girls pretending they didn't like sitting on the fellows' knees : in faſt, row enough to waken Moses ; but no harm done, till that little baggage Patsy ſtarted her games. If ever there's trouble it's always women are at the bottom of it. I can see her now : a regular bad lot she was, with her hot brown eyes and a pointed face like a cat. She could purr when it suited her, you bet, and she could scratch too. She had been doing a deal of purring that evening at young Tom, who was more than half-seas-over. Well, either to rile Tom or to make a fool of Jonathan, what does she do but goes over to Jonathan and climbs on to his knee. Jonathan didn't mind : not he. It was not so easy to make Jonathan look silly. He juſt put his arm round her and talked to her fatherly-like as if he was talking to a little girl. It was enough to make you split to see him so fatherly and so respectable with that little baggage on his knee : and yet you liked him the better for it, and so did she, seemingly, for she ſtopped her cat-play and began talking to Jonathan quite serious and decent-like. Well, of course, that riled young Tom even more than the other thing, and he jumped up from his chair with his mug in his hand and made for the two of them. Jonathan saw that things were getting serious, so he slid the girl off his knee and got on to his feet. Some of the fellows caught hold of Tom and ſtopped him getting at Jonathan, but, as luck would have it, they left his arms free and he slung his pint-pot across the room and caught Jonathan bang on the forehead. Jonathan went over backwards and, as he fell, the back of his head came a tremendous thump againſt the bench he'd been sitting on. That or the pint-pot knocked him clean out and he lay on the floor like a log.

"The roar of voices dried up as though you'd turned off a tap, and everybody crowded forward to have a look at Jonathan. But I didn't. I didn't want to get mixed up in those sorts of goings-on, so I just lifted the latch and faded away, so to speak, and was soon half a mile down the road. And all the way for the rest of my tramp, and in bed that night, I kept seeing to myself, like a comic face at the pantomime, the daft, helpless look on Jonathan's face when his head came bang against the bench."

"And you never heard," asked the landlord, "whether the chap was killed or not?"

"Didn't I, though?" answered the farmer. "I looked in on my way back two days later and they told me Jonathan was all right and had cleared off next morning. It 'ud take more than that, I reckon, to break Jonathan's head. But I never saw him again. No doubt he took a dislike to the place and didn't go back in a hurry."

The landlord collected the three empty mugs and went to the tap to refill them. When he brought them back, each with a bulging head of foam on it, he pushed one of them towards the schoolmaster and said :

"There's your beer, sir ; now what about your story ? "

"Well," replied the schoolmaster, "like our friend here, I have been in all sorts and conditions of inns and I suppose I can tell as good a story about an inn as another man. The inn I have in mind was—like yours, sir—a lonely one, but I don't know much else about it because I arrived there late at night and left early—yes, as early as possible—next morning. It was perhaps eleven o'clock when I arrived. There was no light visible : the windows stared blankly at the moon : so I was all the more surprised, immediately after I had knocked, to see a light swim under the door and to have the door opened to me by a woman fully dressed. Another woman loomed beside her and they both stood there speechless in the doorway listening to my request for supper and making no movement to admit me till I pushed past them into the room. Then they shut and barred the door and I felt that they had allowed me to come in only because they had not dared to shut me out, for now as they came forward into the lamplight and we gazed inquisitively at each other, their appearance came upon me with a shock. Never have I seen such a pair of frightened scarecrows, and it was I, it seemed, that they were frightened of, for both stared at me with a wild unspoken question in their gaze. The thing was incomprehensible, ridiculous : I felt I must try to soothe them. 'Don't let me alarm you,' I said. 'It's a bit late, I know, but I'm not a ghost.' I had thought that a joking remark would reassure them, but the effect of it was the opposite : it seemed, rather, to freeze them and one of them began to tremble uncontrollably. But at least it had roused them, for the trembling one began raking up the fire while the other set about preparing some supper for me, and soon I was seated at the table before cold meat, bread and beer, in the presence of these two dumb creatures who now sat watching me apprehensively, now drifted aimlessly about the room, like a couple of portentous cats, too agitated, it seemed, to keep still for more than a minute. Suddenly I noticed that the teeth of one of them were chattering as though she were suffering from a chill.

" ' Is anything the matter, missus ? ' I asked her.

" ' No, no, nothing at all,' replied the other in a whisper and tried to smile—a ghastly attempt, because her lips stuck to her teeth as though her mouth were dry and the smile turned into a death's-head grin.

"What, in the name of Providence, was wrong with the place ? I hid my perplexity in talk. I talked and talked to my two unanswering spectators—put up as it were a screen of talk against the horrible silence. I explained to them that I was taking a walking-tour, that I had walked thirty miles that day and was dead tired, and then, having finished my supper, I asked for a bed. The question seemed to stun them, for the two wretched creatures stared at one another in dumb agony. ' Bed ? ' said the one with chattering teeth, ' I don't think we could manage it.' Her voice was a terrified whisper. The idea of my staying the night seemed to paralyse her. She turned her drawn face to me, and suddenly my heart melted. ' Don't worry, missus,' I said. ' If I make up the fire a little I shall be quite comfortable down here.' But that seemed to make matters worse.

" ' No ! No ! ' she began tremulously, as though my suggestion were a terrible threat : ' No, not here ! ' Then the other woman broke in :

" ' It's all right,' she said. ' We'll manage a bed for you ' : and she stole out of the room, and after some whispering in the passage a wheezing of loose boards crept up the wall and I gathered that she had gone upstairs to prepare me a room.

"A wind was getting up. It came in sudden gusts, rattling the door and the window-frames, and at every gust the remaining woman started as if she had been struck. 'What's wrong, missus,' I tried again. 'Is there anyone ill in the house?'

"'Ill?' she answered with a gasp. 'No. What makes you ask?' Tired as I was, her reply irritated me. Was there nothing I could say to these hopeless creatures without frightening them into fits? The easiest thing was to remain silent. But the deathly silence that fell between us was broken before long, thank God, by renewed creakings on the stairs and the other creature came tiptoeing into the room and told me that my bed was ready and that she would take me up. She led me upstairs and a few paces down a passage to the right. The first door on the left was mine. Beyond it I noticed another door and, in the opposite wall, midway between the two doors, a wide window reaching almost to the floor whose heavy curtains were undrawn.

"The bedroom was decent enough. 'I advise you,' said my guide in a whisper, 'to keep your window shut. If you open it in a wind like this, all the doors and windows in the house'll start rattling and nobody'll get a wink of sleep.' With that she left me and I was soon in bed.

"But I did not go to sleep. The fact was that I had overtaxed my walking powers and I was too tired to sleep. I lay for perhaps an hour and a half, listening to the wind flustering in the chimney and the whole crazy house creaking and straining like a ship in a storm. Then through these sounds I fancied that I heard another, a slow, dull, rhythmic sound. I strained my ears and it ceased : I slackened my attention and it came again—slow, dull, with sometimes a sharper metallic ring in it. You know how, when you are sleepless, you feel sometimes as if your sense of hearing were tuned up like a fiddle-string and you lie naked and undefended, so to speak, at the mercy of every small sound in the world. That is how I was feeling, and that dull sound hidden away in all the louder noises began to get on my nerves more than all the rest put together. Was it real or was it imaginary ? It never became definite enough for me to decide. At laſt I could ſtand it no longer and got out of bed and cautiously opened the window. The noise was real enough : it was the noise of digging and it came from round the corner of the house. I shut the window and got back into bed, but ſtill not to sleep, for now my reason got to work on the noise. What did it mean ? What could they be up to, digging in the middle of the night ? I thought out elaborate explanations, and all the time I became wider and wider awake. Then I remembered the large window in the passage. I got up again, opened and closed my door noiselessly, and sneaked to the window. A wild moon gleamed and faded and gleamed again in a ſtream of flying clouds. There was no need to open the window this time : by pressing my face to the pane and looking obliquely to the left, I could see a long heap in the garden on the top of which a dark objeſt about the size of a crow hopped up and down every four seconds or so. Then the moon came out and I saw that what had seemed to be a hopping bird was simply a spadeful of soil flung up at regular intervals by an unseen digger. But the reason of this midnight gardening was as unexplained as before. Suddenly my intereſt in the thing vanished and I realized that I was intensely weary. The expedition into the cold passage had cleared my brain and made me ready for sleep. But, as I turned to go, I was aware of another noise—indoors, this time—a measured creaking on the ſtairs. At once all my nerves tightened. I seemed to be liſtening with my whole body. Yes, it was a muffled tread coming slowly up, up, up. I should not be able to reach my door in time, so I ſtepped up on to the wide low window-sill and flattened myself behind one of the curtains. The footſteps reached the ſtairhead and then my heart began to beat in my throat till I felt that the whole house muſt hear it, for the ſteps had turned in my direction. They paused—at my bedroom door, I thought—and I heard the click of a bolt. Evidently I was being bolted in. Then the progreſsion began again. You could hardly call it footſteps : it was a sort of measured shuffling. Could it be an animal ? Or perhaps a lunatic ? I thrilled with horror at the thought. It was passing my curtain. It was as if thick cloth shoes were shuffling along the boards, and I heard the little splinters in the boards catching and breaking in the cloth. Then they came into my field of vision. There were two of

them : two men, one behind the other, shuffling
along towards the second door. They must
have wound sacking round their boots. They
opened the door and went in. I dared not
leave my curtain for fear I should be heard,
for they had left the door open behind them.
In the room I heard the shuffling of their feet
stop, and then the sound as of the dragging of
a heavy sack : a pause, and then once more
the sack was dragged : a stifled whisper . . .
another . . . and then the rhythmic shuffling of
feet began again, but slower, much slower, this
time. The sound of it grew suddenly clearer
and a shadow loomed out into the passage. He
came slowly, and as he emerged into the faint
light of the window I saw that he was coming
backwards way. I stiffened with terror. That
slow shape moving backwards looked so uncanny,
so horribly irrational. The other shape was
following him. Above the shuffle of their feet
I could hear their heavy breathing. A streak
of moonlight slid up the wall and almost at once
the first figure moved into it and I saw that
between them they were carrying a long heavy
sack. Then, as they advanced, the sack was
illuminated section by section as it flowed slowly
through the strip of moonlight, and just as the

light reached the end of the sack, and just before the second man walked into it, a white face, suddenly illuminated, blazed coldly up at me, the mouth hanging crookedly open and the head lolling helplessly on one side, as though the neck that supported it were boneless.

"It was a matter of a second—as quick as taking a photograph—and then the other man had passed through the brightness and the moonlight dropped back on to the blank wall.

"I was up early next morning, but not so early as the woman with the chattering teeth who asked me tremulously if I had slept well. 'Like a top,' I assured her and lifted a weight off the poor soul's mind.

"As I left the inn I glanced over the hedge into the garden. A young fellow was still at work with a spade : he was scattering gravel, and his face looked as if he had been at Death's door. 'Just gravelling the paths,' he said, as he caught my eye.

"That was the end of it," concluded the schoolmaster. "I never heard anything more of the matter from that day to this."

The landlord, who throughout this story had sat immovable, now stirred in his chair. "Pretty gruesome story, that!" he said : and then, turning to the farmer : " I dare say you could tell a queer ſtory or two about this inn of mine if you had a mind to."

" I dare say I could," answered the farmer, " but you don't want ſtories of that kind to get about."

" Why not ? " said the landlord. " The paſt's the paſt. Every one knows the place is reſpeſtable now, and I don't care what's known about happenings here before I took over."

Was it something in the landlord's words, some ſignificance, perhaps, in his mention of " happenings here," which caused the farmer and the schoolmaſter to turn a searching gaze on one another, as though each were upon the brink of an unforeseen revelation ? And when the farmer looked across to the landlord, he saw that he too was glancing eagerly and expeſtantly from one to the other of them.

" You don't care ? " he said to the landlord. " Very well ; then I may as well tell you and this gentleman here that, as a matter of faſt, my ſtory about Long Jonathan happened here."

" I thought as much," answered the landlord. " And, what's more," he said, turning to the schoolmaſter, " I fancy your ſtory happened here, too."

"How did you guess?" replied the school-master.

"Why," said the landlord, "because last summer, when we were putting in a drain through the garden, we dug up your fellow in the middle of the path. And," he added, turning to the farmer, "we dug up not only him but also the remains of his fiddle, and, besides that, he was still wearing one of his gold earrings. The other one we never found."

Interview with a Genius

IT WAS NOT WITHOUT APPREHEN-sion that Overton found himself waiting, as the representative of an important newspaper, in the study of the venerable poet whose work, and especially the great tragedy *Lady Jane Grey*, had roused the enthusiasm of Europe and America. His apprehensions were not unfounded, for the poet's impatience of visitors, his irritability, the strangeness of his opinions, were notorious. But apprehension was presently cut short by the great man himself.

He was a fine figure as he stood for a moment with his hand on the door-knob, almost filling the doorway. The knees were slightly bent, but he held his body erect and the head was proudly set on broad shoulders. A great wave of white hair broke from the right over the left side of his brow. His eyes were large, dark, and gave the impression of never winking ; his face clean-shaved ; the lower lip thrust forward with a determination which was almost truculent. He greeted Overton equally without effusion or coldness.

Overton opened the conversatio n—tactfully, he thought—by telling him that an eminent historian with whom he had recently discussed him, had said that he regarded *Lady Jane Grey* as a valuable contribution to history.

"Indeed," he replied, "I am surprised to hear it."

"Then you did not try," ventured Overton, "to make the play historically correct?"

"The play is a study of personality. I took the fragmentary facts which history has recorded of Lady Jane Grey, and out of them I imagined a personality—one of the infinite number of personalities which might be imagined. But I do not flatter myself that my Lady Jane Grey bears the smallest resemblance to the actual Lady Jane Grey, nor, if it could be proved that she does, would the fact interest me."

"I gather, then, that you are not interested in historical personalities."

"There is no such thing. Fragmentary information about dead personalities survives, but personality itself dissolves irretrievably at the moment of death. It is absurd to pretend that the real Lady Jane Grey exists for us. And even if, in some unthinkable way, her personality were to have survived, it would appear to our twentieth-century eyes as something different from what it really was. We could not hope to see it in its reality without literally transporting ourselves back into the society and intellectual climate in which she lived. But that climate and society no longer exist : an imperfect skeleton only, distorted by our modern vision, survives in literature. Besides which, man cannot, unfortunately, move backwards through time." A silence followed which the poet showed no disposition to interrupt.

"I had hoped," ventured Overton, "that you would allow me to put some questions to you."

"Well," came the reply : "*out* with them."

"I fear that some of them may be indiscreet."

"I thought that to be indiscreet was the first qualification in your profession. What you mean to say is that you fear that I shall realize how indiscreet they are and shut up altogether. Set your mind at rest. Ask what you please : I shall answer or not as *I* please."

"Then I should like to put a question about the *Sonnets to Catherine*. You know, of course, that they are a great problem both to your critics and your biographers. More than half-a-dozen writers have devoted whole books to the subject."

"'I have not read them. I am interested in myself as seen by myself but not as seen by others. Have you ever seen yourself in a convex mirror ? It is curious, but not gratifying. Why do they bother themselves about the subject ? "

"Some of them merely for biographical reasons. They ask, indiscreetly enough, if the sonnets are addressed to your wife, or, if not, to which lady either of those with whom it is common knowledge that you were at various times familiar, or those others who have been deduced, extracted, and, as it were, reassembled, after a patient scrutiny of your writings. One ingenious writer has pointed out that in the year in which the sonnets were published you were spending much of your time with Caterina Borsi."

"That is true. But it happens that I was never in love with that remarkable woman. And it happens also that the sonnets were written, though not published, two years before I met her. But if I had written them while Signorina Borsi was in England, you might have concluded infallibly from that fact that I was not in love with her : or, conversely, if you had certain evidence that I was in love with her this would prove conclusively that the sonnets were not written at that time. When I was in love I had something better to do than write poetry. So much for biography."

"But that is not all. For your critics the question raises a very important point. For if, as some hold, the sonnets were addressed to an actual lady, you remain, as you have already shown yourself in your other works, a great subjective artist ; but if, as one of your critics has said, 'they had no origin in personal experience,' if they are ideal creations, then we must reckon you 'among the greatest objective or dramatic artists.' "

"If I tell you the truth—which in this case I propose to do—it will not be of the slightest help in solving the problem you have just stated. That problem is insoluble because it does not exist, and it does not exist because it is founded on false distinctions. Ask your critic how it is possible for a man to write a poem which does not originate in personal experience. Ask him to make a collection of such poems. I should be interested to see them. Ask him at the same time to make another collection of poems which are not ideal creations. The *Sonnets to Catherine*, so far from being addressed to nobody," said the great man emphatically, and I felt that I was on the brink of a unique, an epoch-making revelation, " are addressed to so many women that it would be impossible for me to tell you their names. My wife, my mother, and all my sisters are among them."

Overton felt that they would be more comfortable on less intimate ground, and, ransacking his mind for some philosophical idea with which the poet had identified himself, he remembered the great *Ode to Death*, that profoundly thoughtful poem in which, never sacrificing poetry to philosophy, the poet had embodied his disbelief in a personal immortality.

" Your views on survival after death," began Overton, " are well known."

" You astonish me," said the poet.

" Yes," maintained Overton, " the *Ode To Death* is one of the best known and most appreciated of all your poems."

" That may be. But you are wrong in supposing that it represents my views. The very fact that it was composed by me makes it impossible that it should do so any longer : in fact, in any attempt to discover my views, the views displayed in that poem are precisely the ones which ought to be left out of account. A work of art, so far as it represents its author, does so only during the process of composition. The moment the poet has perfected his poem it is as though he had dropped it from the window of an express train. The poet goes on, the poem lies immovable, and the spot where it lies is precisely the one spot on earth on which, in whatever direction he may be travelling, the poet himself cannot be. If I were to tell you my views on the subject now, the very fact of my formulating them would cause a change in my position, so that the views that I had just presented to you would at once, strictly speaking, cease to represent me."

" If that is the case, I fail to see how your admirers are ever to arrive at your thought."

" Why should they try to ? Cannot they be content with the images of beauty which I have created ? But if they must burrow after my thought, let them consider that all thought discoverable in my poetry is thought which I no longer think. Let them deduct it from the infinite varieties of thought which I may think, and so diminish by one the infinite number of guesses open to them. I can suggest no better method."

When Overton rose to depart, the old man shook his hand with a sudden fierce cordiality

—the cordiality of the cat towards the mouse— and Overton took his leave, not daring to say " Good afternoon " lest he should irritate the venerable man into asserting that, so far from being afternoon, it was to-morrow morning.

A Dog's Life

THAT ALL FOUR MEN OF THE party were intellectuals is sufficient to account for the fact that the departure of the ladies from the dining-table did not coincide with a series of excursions into gay impropriety. Yet two of them, at least, would have disclaimed the title of intellectual—Lord Brymer, the host, who regarded an intellect as only one item of many in the equipment of a gentleman, and James Fane the poet, who was never tired of proclaiming a profound mistrust of the intellect. Tweed also, the aged and distinguished collie-dog, proudly ignored such trifles and kept his own counsel when the conversation became philosophical. Addington, the philosopher, declared that Tweed was the only genuine non-intellectual, for both Lord Brymer and Fane had succeeded in limiting or repudiating the intellectual solely by a strenuous exercise of intellect. He himself, he said, and Curd, the biologist, were the only members of the party wise enough and honest enough to recognize and accept our inescapable subservience to it.

"Do we appreciate port intellectually?" asked Lord Brymer. "Try, Addington! This is '68." Lord Brymer passed the decanter : the philosopher filled his glass and raised it to his lips.

"A superb wine," he said. "Unofficially, Brymer, I regard the drinking of a port like this as of infinitely greater importance than any philosophy."

·" And I think you will find," said Lord Brymer, " that it is capable of influencing your philosophy. Before we join the ladies, Addington, you will have become a curious blend of Hedonist and Idealist."

" I have no doubt of it," admitted Addington, " and for that reason I should like, at once, to announce my sober conviction that we are all, willy-nilly, intellectualists. The fact that we possess a language is alone enough to prove it, for language is a logical instrument and the rich and elaborate languages used by highly civilized races have developed in response to the need of expressing intellectual facts and intellectual processes of greater and greater subtility. Language is the instrument of intellect : to attempt to rescue it from intellect is to plunge into anarchy and confusion."

Curd, the biologist, while confessing to a lively appreciation of the '68, maintained that

he himself was the only thorough-going intellectual present. "Science," he said, "is at
present in a peculiarly strong position, for in
science alone can we state exactly and uncom-
promisingly what we mean ; even philosophy
cannot do that yet."

"Not perhaps so easily," admitted Addington,
"because we have, as yet, no universally accepted
philosophical terminology : but when once we
have, we shall have little difficulty in making
our terms define our meanings."

"I doubt it, Addington," remarked Lord
Brymer, "and for these two reasons. First,
that no word has an identical meaning for any
two persons. Differences of opinion and association give to every word a private and individual
meaning for each separate human being. The
simplest phrase you utter can never, unfortunately, mean for me exactly what you intend it
to mean. Second, that philosophy never completely knows what it *does* mean. Its inability
to express itself clearly is at least as much the
fault of what it tries to express as of the inex-
actitude of the medium in which it has to express
it. The trouble with you and your like, Addington," and Lord Brymer passed the port once
again to his neighbour, "is that you insist on

trying to express emotional and imaginative convictions in the language and by the methods of science. You are poets without the courage of your convictions."

"Hear, hear!" came from Fane, the poet, who, till then, had been smilingly and speechlessly sipping his port and now filled his glass from a new decanter which the butler had just placed before him.

"I am glad to hear, Fane," laughed Lord Brymer, "that the '68 has at last loosened your tongue. The way in which you have left me to the mercy of these two intellectuals is inexcusable."

"My dear Brymer," answered the poet, "it would have been the blackest ingratitude to you and this wonderful wine to withhold my full attention from it by indulging in cerebral gymnastics, and if I spoke just now it was not because I intended to join in an unprofitable argument but simply because I obeyed the prompting of your '68."

"My '68," said Lord Brymer, "is guaranteed to loosen any tongue. It has frequently obtained for me racing tips and valuable political information otherwise inaccessible. Continue, Fane! Let the wine have its way. Addington has said that you are really an intellectual who is not honest enough to admit it."

Tweed, who lay on his left side, gave three little whimpering barks. He was dreaming of a rabbit-hunt.

"If I were to argue," said Fane, "I should at once be allowing Addington's contention. I meet it with a flat contradiction."

Tweed suddenly sat up, wide awake, and raised one ear.

"I have an intellect, of course," Fane went on, "and I use it ; just as I have a palate and a stomach which I should be using now if Curd would be kind enough—thank you, Curd !—to pass me the decanter. But in the more important matters of life I leave intellect to the engineer, the merchant, and the housekeeper. Listen ! Isn't that a nightingale ? How does intellect help the nightingale, Curd ? "

"It doesn't, Fane. But, though your poetry is not bad, you are not a nightingale. If only you had grown up, you would probably have become a philosopher, perhaps even a scientist. As it is, you drown your philosophy and science in a beautiful emotional confectionery. And I will admit," he added, twirling his glass, "that in my present delightfully abnormal state—

thank you, just the least little drop more—I am foolish enough to prefer them in their disguise."

" That, I think," said Fane, " scores a point to me, for I am at least consistent. Drunk or sober, my opinions are the same, whereas yours change with the contents of your stomach. So do Addington's. Look at him ! Brymer's prophecy has already come true." Addington smiled blissfully across at them and contented himself, for reply, with a vague and airy gesture. " Addington's philosophy, you see," went on Fane, " is purely relative. So is the meaning of words. What Brymer said about language is perfectly correct. No amount of defining and standardizing will improve matters unless you also standardize the brains and environment of every soul who uses it. Each word is a symbol for a fact and, so far, has a meaning common to everybody ; but each individual's reaction to the word and the fact is a private and personal reaction. Fortunately art shows us a way out of this dilemma. We poets use words emotionally and not intellectually. We do not pretend to tell our readers what we mean, but when we express our feelings in symbolical form we construct a potential poem, a thing, that is, which becomes a poem—a private and personal poem—

for each reader. So, if it is a question of scientific accuracy, I am the only accurate one among you, for I say not only what I mean but also what each one of my readers means. I do not use words as labels, but as forces. I make each man express his own truth for himself, and so to each I am as accurate and unmistakable as Tweed is when he barks, for Truth, like everything else, is relative."

Tweed, who had carefully followed the poet's speech, now rose to his feet and, sauntering towards Fane with wagging tail, laid his muzzle on his knee.

"Tweed," said Lord Brymer, "is, I believe, the only completely wise one among us. Even you, Fane, have been human enough to contradict, if not to argue. But Tweed has one point in which he is our inferior. He does not appreciate my '68."

"Indeed?" questioned Addington. "But I don't suppose that Tweed has been given an opportunity of doing so. Personally I find it difficult to believe that there exists a creature so base as not to appreciate this superb wine, and I venture to think," he continued, holding his glass to one of the candles and critically observing the lustrous ruby which half filled it, "I venture to think that if Tweed were invited to taste it he would have something to tell us about it."

"You are right, Addington," said Lord Brymer : "Tweed has not tasted my '68 and it is very possible that I am maligning the dog." Thereupon Lord Brymer emptied his finger-bowl into that of his neighbour and, pouring into it a very liberal draught of port, invited Tweed to step up and try it. The others some-what unsteadily rose from their seats and went round to watch.

"I think it would be more proper, Tweed," said Lord Brymer, "if you were to sit up to the table like a gentleman." A chair was drawn up and Tweed very seriously took his seat upon it. The four men watched him solemnly. He tasted the port, seemed for a moment puzzled then delighted by the flavour, and forthwith applied himself assiduously to finishing it up. Then he sat, surveying his fellow epicures with extreme gravity.

"And now, Tweed," said Lord Brymer, "you will perhaps give us your views on this matter of language and the intellect."

"With pleasure," answered Tweed in a clear and rather pleasant voice.

The guests uttered a united exclamation of
astonishment, but Lord Brymer held up his
hand.

"You are surprised?" he said. "And yet
I told you that my '68 would loosen any tongue.
I confess that I should have been disappointed
if Tweed had not replied. But we are interrupting him. Pray go on, Tweed."

"I can best explain my views," began Tweed,
clearing his throat, "by simply giving you a
brief sketch of the history of the dog civilization.
Many thousands of years ago, the various races
of dogs lived together in vast and highly orga-
nized kingdoms : they possessed an elaborate
and singularly efficient system of trade, waged
extensive and devastating wars, and communi-
cated with one another by means of languages
(and consequently literatures, sciences, and philo-
sophies) infinitely more subtle and extensive
than any known to man. You would all agree
that such a state of things represents a very high
degree of civilization, but you may be surprised
to hear that according to our way of thinking
(which, I must point out, is based on long
experience) it is precisely the reverse. It is,
for us, crude, complicated, unevolved, a primitive
state from which we have slowly and painfully

developed into the state in which you know us. It is thousands of years since our scientists and philosophers decided that the whole of civilization, as we regard it, depends upon the possession of a clear and accurate language. Given that, all other blessings accrue naturally. And so the race of dogs got to work on its language, cutting out indefinite and obscure words, excluding synonyms, accumulating round the words retained a vividness, richness, and reality of meaning acquired from the mass of discarded words which had previously shared and diluted their significance. In three or four centuries our language had been enriched by the cancellation of over two million words. Still the perfecting of the language continued. Careful psychological investigation showed that true meaning was in the last analysis nothing more than the accurate expression of pleasure and pain, love and hate, approval and disapproval, boldness and fear, and a few other pairs which, as some of us believe, will ultimately be made, by more accurate definition and deeper psychological understanding, to coalesce into a single contrasted pair. As our wise men had foreseen, the purification of language resulted almost automatically in the purification of society. The complexities of life

were gradually eliminated : art, which is nothing
but an artificial attempt to enhance the joy of
life, gradually died out as life itself became
more and more completely satisfying. One of
the greateſt advances occurred when, many centuries ago, after the limit of simplification seemed
to have been reached, our wise men decided to
relieve the race even of the trouble of securing
food and shelter. This they did by the simple
device of imposing this task upon the human
race which, about this time, was coming into
prominence.

" As you see us now, we are not far from
the summit of civilization. Mankind provides
us with food, shelter, warmth, and what entertainment we need : in the case of our beſt
families, it even arranges our marriages for us.
We have abolished warfare : the comparatively
rare speƈtacle of a dog-fight in your ſtreets is
the only surviving trace of this barbarous habit.
Under our simple mode of exiſtance a dog can
lead an almoſt perfeƈt life, a life, that is, consiſting in the enlightened enjoyment of the
physical processes as they succeed one another in
his body. Thought and intelleƈtual processes,
except of the simpleſt and moſt praƈtical kind,
have happily been eliminated ; for, as every one

knows, they are only a means to an end, and as the end is achieved the means becomes unnecessary. We have evolved a highly civilized and compact language of barks, growls, howls, and whines, consisting of not more than some fifty simple and almost perfectly expressive vocables, but I still look forward to the day when we shall have reduced language to two opposite terms, expressible respectively by the syllables *bow* and *wow*. Then at last we shall be able to express the subtlest and most complicated meanings with absolute accuracy."

Having completed this remarkable discourse, Tweed jumped to the floor, curled himself on the hearthrug, and was soon asleep, while the human members of the party joined the ladies.

The Materialist

AT LAST THE SERVICE WAS OVER and Mr. and Mrs. Wadsworth emerged into the brilliant sunshine of the churchyard and took the path leading to the wicket that opened into their own garden. It was always a critical occasion and demanded the most delicate manipulation on both sides. For this was the only Sunday in the year on which Mr. Wadsworth went to church and he did this solely to humour Mrs. Wadsworth : so that after the ceremony there was a certain tensity in the situation. Mr. Wadsworth's temper had been severely tried. This yearly homage to convention and Mrs. Wadsworth seemed to him absurd, yet Mrs. Wadsworth, he could see, set great store by it, and he was willing to sink his own inclinations since by doing so he could give her so much happiness. But again, the very fact that it should make her happy vexed him, because it showed so clearly that she could not value his motives for not going to church. Yet Mr. Wadsworth's motives were not trivial : they were deeply sincere, so sincere that he did not even claim reason for them. Anti-Goddite though he was, he was accustomed, in all the profounder problems of life, simply to follow an intuition in which he trusted completely, and what more, after all, did the Goddites, with their *conscience*, profess to do ? For Mr. Wadsworth, whatever that intuition rebelled against was wrong, whatever it approved was right : he had seen too much of the fallibility of human logic to allow it supremacy in ultimate things. Evidently then Mr. Wadsworth could boast a faith as unswerving as the best of the Goddites, and it was Mrs. Wadsworth's low estimation of his faith that wounded him. Not that she expressed or even realized her attitude, but this exaction of yearly tribute implied it quite unmistakably. And so Mr. Wadsworth was aware on the way home of a strong impulse to make sarcastic and profane remarks about the service : he felt vaguely that only by so doing could he readjust the balance so monstrously upset by this annual distortion of himself, and it required all his strength of mind to refrain, indeed he could only do so by refraining from speech altogether. As for Mrs. Wadsworth, poor lady, she clung desperately to this yearly concession, for she had the conviction that if she could ensure his going to church even only once a year, he would be saved from the terrible fate of all disbelievers :

and each year as they left the church she longed to ply him with questions about his impressions of the service in the blind hope of eliciting some sign of grace from him. And she, too, had to exercise incredible self-restraint in order to refrain, for to do otherwise, her good sense told her, would be to provoke inevitable disaster. But one of them must say something, for, as they walked together down the path, the silence was rapidly becoming absurd.

" The sermon was a little long," she ventured indulgently.

Mr. Wadsworth instantly exploded. " The sermon was infernally long, Elizabeth, and as arrant nonsense as I have heard these ten years." Then, relieved by this outburst, he regained control of himself. What a beast he was ! He was only hurting her feelings. And, as another silence began to accumulate he made a supreme effort.

" The choir has improved, Elizabeth ; they sang the hymns well . . . in fact, admirably." That *admirably* almost choked him, and he remained silent until they reached the house, remembering with acute discomfort how, as they entered the church, he had seen the deadly eye of the Vicar's wife duly register his arrival, and

how insufferably, as they came out of it, the
pious Miss Mott had smiled at him—the smile
of a saint welcoming a rescued sinner. " A
detestable prig," he muttered to himself. But
to Mrs. Wadsworth that small commendation of
the choir had been sufficient. She felt happy
and secure about him now and the charming
smile on her face drew one from his as they
entered the house. . . .

He shut away their prayer-books into the hall
drawer and hurried upstairs to change his infected
clothes. He undressed with fury, although there
was not the smallest reason for hurry, and got
out his most disreputable clothes. As he pulled
them on, he felt that he was reassuming his
normal personality, and feeling freer and cooler
he went downstairs.

In the hall his wife patted him on the back.
It was a near thing : he felt his ill-temper boil
up dangerously like milk in a pan. How unreasonable, how false the whole situation was !
Why did she insist on perpetuating it year after
year, instead of letting him go his own way, as
he let her go hers ? Each year it brought this
uncomfortable constraint into their otherwise
harmonious relations. But, as he took his old,
greasy hat from the hall table and felt it settle

easily and softly round his head, his temper
subsided without boiling over. A warm puff
of rose-scented air came from the open door and
at once a wave of contentment broke over him.
He took his wife's arm and they went together
into the garden. . . .

One afternoon, a few days later, Mr. Wadsworth crossed the hall with his sketching materials.
" If you want me, Elizabeth," he called to his
wife, " you will find me in the church, sketching."

Since his visit to church, Mr. Wadsworth
noticed that various beautiful details of the
church kept rising again and again to the surface
of his mind. He thought of the lovely thir-
teenth-century glass in the East window, the
Norman chapel on the right of the choir, the
delicately carved canopy of the tomb opposite
to it. But, as if to something which included
and symbolized them all, his mind returned
with a still deeper wonder and delight to
the old well under the altar which had been
a sacred place long before the church had
been built or Christianity had been brought
to Britain. Then these constantly recurring
thoughts grew into an irresistible desire to
sketch those things, and, following his usual

habit, Mr. Wadsworth immediately obeyed the impulse.

For three days he worked away with pencil and brush and at the end of that time it became clear to him that he did not really want to sketch these things at all. No, he saw perfectly now that his desire had been simply to be in the church, to have all its beautiful details about him and to take them. somehow, into his mind ; and now he realized unmistakably that he had invented the sketching merely as an excuse for going into the church. From that moment Mr. Wadsworth ceased to sketch, but he kept his sketching things before him, for how, otherwise, could he, if he were discovered, account for his presence there ? People go to church for religious, artistic, or antiquarian reasons and for no other reason whatever. But he was there for none of these reasons : his reason for being there was not definable.

Next day things had become even more transparent in his mind. He felt still as he had always felt about the customary forms of worship and belief : the thought of his annual attendance at the service was no less irritating, but now he was aware that as he sat alone in the church he was in communion with a certain current of life.

Spiritual, supernatural ? His mind vigorously denied it. He did not believe in the spiritual or the supernatural. For him the universe was a material universe, and the material, the physical, was the only reality. But it was precisely with reality that Mr. Wadsworth felt himself to be in touch as he sat in the church. He seemed to be experiencing not a refutation of his materialistic theory of life, but a deeper confirmation of it. He was, he felt, in touch with the humanity, the sum of human delight and human effort, which had created the church, the Norman chapel, the glass of the East window, and, long before that, had venerated the sacred well. To enter the church was to immerse himself in that humanity and become part of it.

And then, as his emotions defined themselves yet more clearly, he became conscious of a longing to take part in formal acts. He was strongly impelled to cross himself, to walk up the nave with arms extended upwards, to fall down in reverence before the altar-stone which covered the well. It was the acts themselves which he desired : the accepted significance of them did not interest him, indeed he felt a strong antipathy to it. But the acts, the gestures themselves, seemed to answer some profound

239

need in his emotional life. What did it mean ?
He could not tell, but, though unexplained, the
fact existed none the less : evidently then they
possessed some deep and hidden efficacy. Mr.
Wadsworth had always been completely frank
with himself. It was his frankness, his refusal
to submit to any compromise in his mental
attitude to life, which had made him throw over
what he had been brought up to call religion :
and now, with no sense of doing anything unreasonable, he was ready to admit the value of these
seemingly mysterious acts when once he was
sure of their emotional appeal. He went to the
door and turned the key in the lock. There
was no doubt or shame in his mind at what he
was going to do, but he knew that if he were
seen he would be misunderstood, that it would
be thought either that he was mad or that he
had come over to the Goddites. He knew that
he would never be able even to make Elizabeth
understand.

Then, when the door was locked, he walked
up the nave, passed under the rood-screen, and
in an ecstasy of delight and liberation flung
himself on the stone floor before the altar. . . .

As he came out of the porch into the churchyard a bell began to ring and he was shocked

to meet Miss Mott coming in. "There is a service in ten minutes," she said politely.

"Yes," replied Mr. Wadsworth, "I have just escaped in time, haven't I?"

Miss Webster's Dream

ONE WAS ATTRACTED TO POOR Miss Webster not so much by what she was as by what she was meant to be, what she was always just failing to be, and it struck me now that her attitude, as we sat together on the terrace of the hotel overlooking a huge expanse of blue Mediterranean, was typical of the failure that she was, for she sat with her head drooped a little to one side in the attitude of one who has been crying, and her hands lay empty on her lap. Yes! That was the impression: her hands were not merely resting; they were empty, "as if," I said to myself, "the cup of life had been snatched from them."

It was not that Miss Webster had no interests: she had many. Music, painting, embroidery, architecture—in all these things she was interested, in her dry, prim way. She even did a little harmless sketching herself. But when she spoke of these hobbies one was aware of something cold and impersonal—one might almost say, something tasteless—in her appreciation, as though the salt of life had been left out of it. And indeed it seemed, in other respects, as if life did not interest her, for of people, animals, flowers, the open, physical out-of-doors she seldom spoke. I tried to picture Miss Webster in love, Miss Webster bathing in the Mediterranean, even Miss Webster dancing a *pas seul*. It could not be done. The impulse which instigates such things had, one felt, been dried out of her. My thoughts turned inevitably to old Mrs. Webster. She had not left her room all day, and I found myself wondering whether Miss Webster's lot was perhaps a little happier on such days, when she had at least a few small intervals of respite, even though the continual running to and from her mother's room was more tiring than simply talking or reading to her on the terrace. And suddenly I felt angry with the domineering, selfish old invalid who had reduced Miss Webster to what she was. If only old Mrs. Webster would die, I thought, perhaps even yet Miss Webster might regain her lost humanity. And then I went on to wonder if Miss Webster never wished—if only involuntarily, in her heart of hearts—that old Mrs. Webster would die. I almost hoped that she did : at least, I decided grimly, it would be a sign of grace, a sign that her smothered personality was still alive : and I longed suddenly to have a glimpse into the mind of the poor thwarted creature.

As if in answer to my wish, Miss Webster just then looked up, caught my eye, and glanced timidly aside. "I had such a curious dream last night," she began in her faded voice, "and so vivid that when I woke I could have sketched the scene of it in every detail. . . . I dreamt that I was mounting a wide stone stair, leading to a sort of open loggia. You know Florence? The Bargello? Well, it was something like the stair in the Bargello. When I reached the top, I saw in an alcove to the right a nun seated at a table on which was an illuminated manuscript. I knew, somehow, that she was the Mother Superior. But I paid no more attention to her because there was a little Gothic door on my left which attracted me. It was ajar, so I pushed it open and went in. I found myself in a low, stone-vaulted room with beautiful stained-glass windows. On stools, tables, and chairs lay a great profusion of illuminated manuscripts, the most lovely things you ever saw, and as I went from one to another I felt that illuminating was what I had always wanted to do. A large black crucifix, which rather frightened me, hung between the windows, and the walls were covered with tapestries, each an intricate web of lovely flower-designs, so minute, so perfect, that I can see them still. Among the other furniture I noticed a black cabinet full of little drawers. I went over to it and pulled out a drawer. It was full of butter-flies carefully arranged and labelled, and as I opened drawer after drawer, I found that they all contained these butterflies, gorgeous unknown kinds more beautiful than any I had ever seen."

"But how sad, Miss Webster," I said.

"Sad?" said Miss Webster. "Why sad?"

"Why, because your butterflies were all dead and your flowers all woven flowers, and your room low and stone-vaulted. I wish they had been living butterflies fluttering among real flowers in a sunny garden."

Miss Webster laughed her timid laugh. "How absurd you are," she said. "What difference can it make? It was only a dream. . . . Well, I looked at the butterflies for a long time and at the illuminated manuscripts too, and then I saw a door which I had not previously noticed near the window. I tried it : it was open. It was so low that I had to stoop as I went through it. Inside was a chapel, there was an altar at the far end of it, and on the floor in front of the altar lay . . . what do you think ? "

" A stuffed bird-of-paradise ? " I said.

" No. An open coffin with a young monk in it."

" My dear Miss Webster," I exclaimed, " but how awful."

" No," said Miss Webster, " it wasn't so very awful, because, you see, he was alive."

" Alive, Miss Webster ? And what did he look like ? "

" I don't know," said Miss Webster, " I couldn't see, because his face was turned away from me."

" Then how do you know he was young ? "

" You keep speaking as though the thing were real. I know because . . . well, I just knew, as one does in dreams. . . . After that I returned into the larger room. . . ."

" Leaving your young man ? "

" Leaving the monk : and, crossing the larger room, I came out again on to the loggia. . . ."

" Where your mother was ? "

" My mother ? You mean the Mother Superior."

" To be sure. The Mother Superior."

246

"Yes, and the Mother Superior was still there in the alcove, so I thought I would go and see what she was illuminating. But when I got nearer I saw . . . it really was rather dreadful this time. . . ."

"You saw that she was signing death-warrants?"

"You keep interrupting," said Miss Webster. "No, of course I didn't. I saw that the foot which showed under her robe was a skeleton foot, and when I looked into her face it was the face of a skull."

"And of course you woke up terrified?"

"No, I was not terrified, somehow. On the contrary, I was delighted, and I clapped my hands and shouted out aloud : 'Then all this belongs to me.'"

"Including the young man?"

"The young . . .? Oh, the monk. No, by that time I had forgotten the monk."

"And then?"

"And then I woke up. Isn't it curious what things one dreams of?"

"Very curious, Miss Webster. But I'm sorry you forgot the young man."

In the Park

GLADYS SAT STARING INTO THE
fire with a magazine on her knee. She had
sat there since dinner and now it was getting on
for tea-time. She had not once opened the
magazine, and her mother, as she passed to and
fro across the room putting away the crockery
and getting the iron ready to iron the washing,
looked at her with disapproval. Gladys was
thinking : not of anything particular, but,
being in a bad temper, as she so often was nowadays, she sat there shutting her mother out,
as it were, and letting the thoughts drift idly
down the stream of her mind. She felt a vague
resentment against her mother and also against
her friends Mildred and Florry. Why she
was angry with her mother she could not have
said, but she was angry with Mildred and Florry
because of their silly talk about young men.
They were always talking about their adventures,
as they called them, and sometimes they whispered secrets—things which, they said, Gladys
would not understand, and then they would
giggle till Gladys could scarcely restrain herself
from smacking their silly giggling faces. Then
they would put embarrassing questions to her.

"Just ask her," Florry would say, "if she's ever been out with a young chap," and when Mildred asked her Gladys always felt her face burn scarlet and stammered something to the effect that some people had other things to do than always to be bothering about young men. She hated those questions because they always made her feel inferior, and she hated them too because she knew that Mildred and Florry were well aware that, as a matter of fact, she never had been out with a young man.

Then suddenly she felt that she could sit there no longer. There was something she wanted, something that would soothe away her sulks and make her feel fresh and serene again. What could it be? Fresh air, perhaps : and she put on her hat and coat—how she hated her hat and her wretched pale face in the glass —and taking the magazine, went out.

But, once in the street, she felt depressed and nervous. Why, after all, had she come out? She would actually have turned back if it had not been less trouble just to drift on from shop-window to shop-window. Then she crossed the street and made for the entrance to the park. It was in the park, she now remembered, that Florry had had one of her silly adven-

tures with a young man. Why she ever bothered
with Mildred and Florry she couldn't imagine.
They were nice enough sometimes, but really,
when you came to think of it, so common. Some
way down the long straight walk that led into
the park from the gates, a seat stood under two
plane-trees, their hanging boughs scantily hung
with great yellow leaves—yellow and brown
kid-gloves, she said—made an intricate dome
above it. Gladys sat down and opened her
magazine. The park was almost deserted, but
occasionally footsteps approached on the gravel,
passed her seat, and died away. Gladys did
not look up when they approached, but listened,
listened with all her ears and a thumping heart,
as she sat with downcast eyes reading and re-read-
ing one paragraph of her silly magazine. At
last, after a longer interval than usual, footsteps
approached once again, but this time when they
came level with the seat they suddenly hesitated.
Gladys's heart beat violently and she glanced
timidly up. Then at once she cast her eyes
down again to her book, retaining a vision of a
round smiling face and very bright blue eyes.
The young man sat down at the other end of
the bench. She did not look up but she heard
him take out a cigarette and matchbox, tap the

cigarette lazily and then light it. It sounded somehow as if he was doing these things in a humorous way, as though each action was a criticism on her exclusiveness, and attempt to attract her attention, rather than a thing done for its usual reason. If she were to look up she fancied that she would find the blue eyes and smiling face looking at her quizzically. But she did not look up : she continued to pretend a profound interest in her wearisome magazine. Then he dropped his stick : she started and had looked up before she knew what she had done, and there were the face and eyes exactly as she had suspected.

" Nice day for the time of the year," said the young man, not as if he meant it but as if he were quite kindly and pleasantly poking fun at her.

" Yes," said Gladys and at once returned to the magazine. Then there was a long silence, broken only by the chirping of two angry sparrows.

" Not 'arf talkative, are you ? " said the voice ; such a pleasant, humorous voice, too. What should she do ? She would have liked to answer him naturally and humorously too, but she was too shy for that. Then, discovering

251

that it had already become too late to answer
at all, she remained silent. That was fatal,
for it put her, in some degree, at the mercy of
the young man, and he, of course, at once continued his chaff.

"Don't know why you're shouting so loud,"
he said : "I ain't deaf." Still Gladys took no
notice. After all, so long as she kept silent she
could not be thought to be encouraging him :
she might simply be absorbed in her magazine.

"Come and hear the silent lady," said the
voice. "Only sixpence entrance. Never spoke
since she was born, and not much then." Gladys
slowly turned a page of her magazine, of which
she had not read a word. An interminable
pause followed during which, though there was
nothing to be heard, Gladys was sure that he
was laughing at her. It was becoming
impossible. With her, the thing had never
been a joke from the beginning : it had begun
in agitation and now she was aware of a growing
tensity in the situation which she would not be
able to bear much longer.

"I say," said the young man, as if a happy
thought had suddenly struck him : "let's go
and have tea. What d'you say if I stand you

a tea ? " But Gladys felt that now nothing
would ever enable her to speak.

"Did you ever ? " said the voice, appealing
to the park in general. Then he changed his
method. " Perhaps if I were to take the magazine away . . ." and he suddenly shuffled his
feet. Instantly Gladys slid away to the end of
the bench and turned her back on him, so that
her legs hung over the end, her toes just touching
the ground and her left arm encircling the back.
She had moved suddenly, with no defined
motive, and, now that she had done so, she
realized that two things had happened : she
had given herself a clear view of the entrance
of the park, so that she could see if any one
approached, and she had also entered into a
very complicated relation with the young man,
for now she had ceased to ignore him, and if
her action had suggested disapproval, her remaining there expressed something little short of
flirtation. Her boldness alarmed her : her
legs began to tremble violently ; she could
hardly resist the impulse to get up and fly. But
a hard, fierce determination held her there and
she slid forward so that her heels touched the
ground and her legs trembled less violently.
The soothing voice began again.

"Well, I never. Not so much as a civil word for a chap when he asks you out to tea. . . . Oh, very well. I'm sure I meant no harm. Still, I don't see as it 'ud be any worse having tea in a public restaurant than sitting on a bench with a feller in a lonely park. . . . I could do with a bit of tea meself. Now what about it? Eh? . . . Well, I never. Lorst your tongue, I suppose. Bit it orf, perhaps, so's not to say thank you when a feller asks you out to tea. Had enough to eat eating your tongue, perhaps! . . . H'm, can't even laugh, much less speak!" The young man sighed. Gladys sat still, clinging to a situation which she felt she was allowing to slip away from her. The moment was coming, she knew, when she would be able to stay there no longer, when she must let go and lose everything. Her staying there seemed to her every moment more impossible, more indecent: and yet she stayed, hoping for . . . she did not know what.

The young man again stirred his feet suddenly and her head shot round. He had not moved from his place but his eyes were waiting for hers and he laughed roguishly, but not with the same light-hearted frankness as before: there was a touch of harshness now—cruelty even. Or was it only unhappiness ? But how bright and blue his eyes were, and his teeth, too, were very good. " Got you that time," he said almost fiercely. She turned her head away quickly. " 'Ere, come orf it," the voice began again. " What are you getting at ? Come on, Missy, be a sport. It's getting late. There's no good going home for tea now, and there's quite a nice place near here. And afterwards we might go to the pictures : and after that, if you found you didn't like me, you could go home."

What did that mean ? If she didn't like him ? And suppose she did : what was the alternative to going home ? Still she remained, her body shuddering, her teeth chattering as if she were cold. She felt tired, and suddenly she hated and despised herself. She had hated Mildred and Florry for their loose talk about young men and now she was just as bad as they —worse, because, though she wanted to get up and go, something bad, something wicked made her stay. She had no illusions about it. She knew it was bad, and also she knew she was determined to stay. She was consciously, deliberately, stubbornly doing what she knew was bad. But now the excitement was going and she was only tired and disappointed. She felt inclined to burst into tears, to turn round and burst into tears on the nice broad waistcoat of the nice young man. What a relief it would be. Everything would immediately become natural again and she would be happy. He shuffled his feet again and at once she was on the defensive, hard, cold, and a little frightened. But she did not look round. She was not going to be caught in that way again. But she listened. Her whole body seemed to be listening. Her back shrank as though at an impending touch. But she heard nothing. She drew in her breath with a little shuddering sob in her throat and stared coldly down the long gravel walk. It was getting dark. She must go. The thing could not be carried on any longer. Suddenly his arm slid round her and gripped her against his body so roughly that she almost cried out, and his face came over her shoulder. She felt his hot, bristly cheek against hers. " Just one," he whispered. " Just a little one," and he put a great wet kiss on her cheek.

Next moment she was hurrying down the path to the gates. Instinctively she had flung out her elbows and wriggled herself free without a word, without a sound. She tried to hurry, but her legs were numb and tingling. Never once looking back, she made straight for the gates. Her only thought was movement, escape. She was terrified, angry both with herself and him, and delighted. And there was another reason too why she did not look back : she had ceased to think of the young man, at least as a distinct individual. Certainly he had been part of the adventure, but it was her adventure which concerned her now, and that she had brought away with her, a thing to be hugged and dreamed of. It had happened : it had actually happened. She was equal with Mildred and Florry now : she too had her own secret. She would not tell them about it. Oh, dear, no. She would merely smile mysteriously when they began their silly talk, and one day, sometime hence, she would let fall a suggestion that she too had adventures like every one else, but . . . well, there was such a thing as restraint : some people did not care to discuss their private affairs with the first comer. Nor, of course, would she tell her mother. After all, grown-up people can't tell their mothers everything : no one could expect it.

Supper was already on the table when she reached home. She felt now that it would be easy to be pleasant with her mother, because now, somehow, she was freed from her.

"Why, Gladys," her mother said, "I thought you were never coming. Running about with Mildred and Florry, I suppose."

"Mildred and Florry?" said Gladys, raising her eyebrows. "Why Mildred and Florry?"

"Why? Because it's always them when you come in late."

"Oh, dear me, no," Gladys replied, with a strange ladylike accent. "I've been by myself, if you want to know. At least, most of the time."

Her mother turned sharply and looked at her. Gladys saw she had been rash. "Well, you can hardly say you're alone when the streets are full of people," she added jocularly, as she took off her coat and hat.

But it was difficult, as it turned out—very difficult, to be either pleasant or unpleasant to her mother. Both at supper and after she had cleared supper away, she could not think of anything to talk about. The room kept going blurred : her thoughts wandered, and she woke up to find her mother in the middle of a sentence. What she wanted was to be alone, to get to bed and dream over her wonderful secret. And when at last she was in bed and the gas out, she flung herself upon her adventure with a sigh of relief, as a miser, when he has locked the door, flings himself upon his gold. When she had undressed, she had found a bruise over one of her ribs where he had gripped her. She would feel that little painful place for days and, each time she felt it, she would remember what had caused it.

How wonderful, how glorious it was. She went over it all again and again—her fear ; her desperate, insistent daring ; her tingling delight. How glad she was that she had forced herself to wait instead of running away at once. Now she was changed completely : she was free, strong, self-possessed. Should she go back to the park to-morrow or the next day ? She was surprised to find, now, that she had a fear, almost a dislike, of the park. No, she had got her adventure safe, indeed she was a little glad that it was over, and for the present the prospect of new adventures did not interest her. Twelve struck, and still she lay awake. She did not mind. She was so content that loss of sleep did not matter. It was a waste to sleep when she had such glowing happiness to remain awake for. She stretched her toes into the cold part of the bed and sighed serenely. A distant motor-horn, distant chimes, a far-barking dog, occasionally broke the long soft hiss of silence. She got out of bed and drew up the blind. A yellow half-moon like a great slice of melon hung low over the roofs and chimney-pots : below her, in the pale gaslight, the street was a vaguely luminous canal. How unearthly, how impossibly still it all looked, as if something had bewitched the familiar view. " Like seeing behind the scenes," she said to herself. And then, on the wall of the backyard, she saw two cats clearly silhouetted. They were about ten feet apart. One, a large dark shape, sat sullenly and stubbornly glaring at the other : and the other—why, goodness gracious, the other was their own little Fluff, and there she was, diligently washing herself and ostentatiously ignoring the other except when, fancying he had moved, she shot a little lightning glance of apprehension at him, and then coldly resumed her provocative toilet.

" Strange things cats are ! " said Gladys as she got back into bed.

The Soft-Hearted Man

ERNLEY REGARDED HIMSELF AS something of a philosopher, not in the professional sense of the term but simply in the sense that he viewed life philosophically and recognized reluctantly that it is useless to try to be too good in an indifferent world. He was a bachelor and enjoyed an income of £500 a year. £500 a year is not much, but it is enough to be philosophical on. Ernley heartily wished that every one had £500 a year, for, besides being a philosopher, he was also, as he would sometimes deprecatingly admit, something of a Socialist, and if any effort of his could have brought it about that every one should have £500 a year, well then, he would have seen to it that they got it—yes, even (he was sure of it) if he had to be the one soul in the world to forgo his £500. But actually—and there is no good disregarding actuality—things are not so simple as that. Nothing that he could do would bring about this desirable state of things : it would come, no doubt, when the nation as a whole was sufficiently enlightened to think as he did and the thing was in consequence established by law ; meanwhile, all he could do was to make the best of things as they were.

And there seemed, to one who took the larger view, so little that one could do. The amount that Ernley could afford to give, with his paltry £500 a year and everything nowadays so expensive, was so infinitesimal that it was as good as nothing. Besides, charity as every one knows who takes the larger view, merely helps to produce acquiescence in an evil state of things and so delays reform.

So Ernley regretfully gave nothing. Moreover—for, besides being a philosopher and a Socialist, he was also (he flattered himself) rather an acute judge of character—if one simply gave, ignorantly, indiscriminately, one might so easily give to the wrong person and thus throw money away, for so many folk one came across who were down on their luck, were so visibly wanting in any qualities that would fit them for a useful place in the general scheme. Look at the average unemployed who grinds a barrel-organ. Look at his face. One recognizes the kind of chap at once : one knew him in the army, the sort of man who was always chattering, arguing, grousing, and, when it came to the point, was always perfectly useless. Look at the usual woman who sells matches : generally a debased, often an obviously drunken type. It was really a matter of natural gravitation : such people remained where they were simply because they were congenitally incapable of being anywhere else. Give any one of them £500 a year and after a year he would be back where he started from. Of course there was unemployment and all that : still, as Ernley always maintained, if a man was really fit for a job he could get it. Statistics are all right, of course, to a certain point, but when you take the larger view statistics are often dangerously misleading.

Still, these people did occasionally bother Ernley. That was the worst of it, he was really such a tender-hearted chap. One evening, as he hurried home to dress for the theatre (he did not really care for the theatre, but unhappily if you belong to a certain class such things are thrust upon you) a woman with a child offered him matches. Ernley ignored her. Not because he was hard-hearted : he would have preferred to stop and speak to her, to refuse politely and kindly or even to buy matches which he did not want. But to buy matches would do so little, so infinitely little, that, to anyone who forced himself to take the larger view, it was as good as nothing : and, after all, if one were to stop and talk and give her a shilling out of sheer sympathy . . . well, the woman simply wouldn't understand. Ernley was not a fool ; in fact, as he always said, he was some- thing of a philosopher and he knew well enough that a woman of that sort would be quite imper- vious to the finer feelings : she would regard him as a " gent," one of a superior class (how Ernley hated these class-distinctions which falsi- fied the attitude of human beings to one another) and she would take the shilling and leave the sympathy, or else, worse still, she would callously deceive him, spin him a yarn and attempt to work on his feelings by false pretences. While such things were possible, the only thing to do, alas, was to do nothing.

But just after he had passed her, after her first whining offer, the woman had added an " Oh, please, sir," as if with a last hope of check- ing him, and there was something in the intonation of that " Oh, please, sir," which really upset Ernley. That was the worst of being such a tender-hearted chap. It really went to his heart. Yet, of course, it was sheer sentimentality. That " Oh, please, sir," was part of the woman's stock in trade : she undoubt-

edly trotted it out a hundred times a day just
as glibly as one says "Don't mention it!"
He thought it over. It was in the single word
"please," he found, that the disquieting intonation lay: the "Oh" and the "sir" were
colourless. Yet every time he tried the phrase
over in his dispassionate analysis of its mechanism, the sting of it was there. Damn it all, it
was going to bother him for the rest of the evening: possibly for days and even weeks. It
almost seemed worth while to turn back and
give the woman something. A bob is not
much to give for one's peace of mind. But no,
really! This was the sheerest sentimentality.
He positively must not let that kind of thing get
hold of him. It was all the effect of the war:
his nerves had never been the same since he got
back from Egypt. But, all the same, how hateful the world was, to be sure! Why couldn't
everybody live together in good fellowship?
As things were, all that a soft-hearted fellow
could do was to take refuge behind a shell of
callousness, or rather of inattention, whenever
he became aware that the outside world was
making an assault upon his feelings.

Ernley had long since adopted this method
of defence and he found that it worked remark-

ably well, so well indeed that he sometimes caught himself wondering a little uncomfortably in what way he differed from the really callous person. But that, of course, was absurd, for was he not perpetually receiving evidence to the contrary? The incident of the woman with the matches was a case in point. Obviously his protective shell was something very different from real callousness, otherwise how was it that her confounded stab—her unforgettable " Oh, please, sir "—had got through? Still that other case, the case of the old lady, was extremely disquieting, although no one could deny that her appearance was against her.

What an extraordinary old parrot she had looked, vaguely waiting for a bus near Piccadilly Circus. Ernley, too, was waiting for a bus. It was about five o'clock, when everybody seems to be waiting for a bus and most of the buses, when they do arrive, are already full. So Ernley had passed the time in watching her and—being a rather acute judge of character—in reconstructing from the evidence before him her habits and personality.

The evidence before him was curious: it consisted of a tall, thin, bony figure, the head

266

pushed forward so that the back was almost hunched. An old black hat, once fashionable and now dowdy, with a broad brim of transparent lace, was set too far back on her head, giving her a slightly drunken look and exposing too completely the face beneath, a face in which cheeks and forehead converged into a great trunk-like nose beneath which it fell away, chinless, into her high lace collar, so that the whole countenance seemed to be bent forward in a sort of comic devoutness. Yes, it was a parrot's face, and the little blear, expressionless eyes were a parrot's. Ernley almost expected to hear her crackle her beak. Her black dress showed the remains of a richness and elegance beyond her means : now it was worn and faded and she had put it on in such a way that the whole thing, from collar to waist, from waist to foot, was twisted. The long plain sleeves of transparent lace were darned : one was beginning to part from the shoulder and near the shoulder of the other the torn frill of a camisole showed through. Even the little bag she carried seemed to have shared its owner's deterioration. To come to town, or rather into the centre of the town, was for her, Ernley observed, an unusual event, for she seemed bewildered, puzzled, by the buses and glared quizzically yet desperately at them with her little expressionless eyes, as if in the fond hope that some sudden intuition would reveal to her the one which would take her back into the rapidly fading, once respectable district where she had lived all her life in the house on the north side of the square. Ernley pictured the house sixty years ago. In those days the windows shone and the paint was fresh, and, like all the other houses in the square, it bore the stamp of well-to-do Victorian respectability. Through its windows one caught glimpses of marble mantel-pieces, coloured flower-pots, and the shining mahogany and horsehair of the furniture. Every Sunday at a quarter past ten the front-door opened and Mamma, Papa, and the two lean daughters emerged, irreproachably dressed, and proceeded in a body to church ; and, by the time they returned, the house was redolent of roast-beef. And once a year, in the summer, a " growler " fantastically encrusted with luggage stood at the door and the same quartet squeezed themselves into it and drove off to the station in costumes which portended the seaside. Then Emily married and Arabella was left alone with the old people and during the next fifteen years she patiently and dutifully saw them out of the world and the house became hers. Her friends considered that she ought to sell and go to live in the country, but Arabella had clung stubbornly to the old place, or rather, the old place had clung to her, wrapped her dry soul in its web until she could not disengage herself. Then began the long process of decay. Slowly, at first imperceptibly, the district, for some complicated sociological reason, began to fade, and Arabella faded with it. After another fifteen years none of the old inhabitants remained : there was hardly anyone left on whom she could call. Her income, too, faded : its purchasing power was seriously diminished : she could only afford one servant now. But still she clung on, protestingly, among the horsehair, the flower-pots and the marble mantelpieces : desperately keeping up appearances. Emily had died ten years ago and now Arabella never left home. All day, Ernley was sure, she sat lonely in her sitting-room, while her little maid sat lonely in the kitchen, for it is a bad thing to allow servants to forget their station. Yet how different life might have been for her if she had been human enough to abandon her absurd gentility ; if she had gone out and made friends "beneath her" (as she would have said) and treated her little maid too as a friend and companion; and, instead of crippling her savings by clinging to a style of dress reminiscent of more prosperous days, if she had descended to a serviceable cloth which, however old, would have remained respectable. Better, thought Ernley, to be the blind man who stood there where the buses stopped, his back to the wall, his tin mug slung in front of him, simple, honest, untroubled by the fictitious complexities of convention, than this foolish old woman, so dislocated, so fantastic, so almost terrible in her panoply of taboos, her desperate class-consciousness, which had slowly sapped her humanity and left her little better than one of those grey, wingless, creeping, light-avoiding creatures that live among wreckage.

It is remarkable, if you accustom yourself to studying character, how much you can learn at first sight. Ernley was really rather struck by his analysis.

But suddenly, as he was watching her, Arabella made a little gesture of distress, and then, like a parrot looking for a seed, began rummaging and peering short-sightedly into her bag—anxiously, hurriedly, as though some sudden accident had occurred in which she believed she could help. Then, with a beautiful pity shining in her absurd mask, her anxious attitude, her wholly unselfconscious manner, she hurried up to the blind man, dropped a shilling into his mug, and said a few words which Ernley could not catch. It was inexplicably, profoundly touching, a thing for adoration and tears. It was as though a world had been destroyed and created again in a new image. Incredible, monstrous, that such a thing should happen in this perfectly reasonable life of lamp posts, buses, stays, parasols, and bowler-hats. Yes, the old lady had certainly got her own back on Ernley. His shell was not merely stabbed, it was shattered. The flimsy pretences of his philosophy, his Socialism, his tender-heartedness, his precious character-reading, crumbled before the clear, spontaneous flood of her humanity, and he saw himself selfish, impertinent, a fool and a coward. The world that he had so glibly created spun back on its axis and he perceived in Arabella's faded finery the sign of a patiently persistent impulse towards beauty and personal refinement, and in the horsehair, the flower-pots, the mantelpieces, symbols of the anxious search for stability, for continuity in the general flux of things—for the warm, rich-memoried, tangible life with which every human being seeks to hide himself from the emptiness of infinity.

Farmer Brock's Funeral

FARMER REED HAD A FINE HERD OF shorthorns, and it was to see a young bull which I thought of buying of him that I took the train down to Dore. After Dore the line runs west with hills on the right and a plain on the left and ends at the coast twenty miles farther on. The station is called Dore Junction, because a little branch-line runs in there from the south out of Dumnel Marsh and links up its scattered farms and villages with the outer world.

At Dore station I found Reed waiting for me in a smart two-wheeled trap and we set off at a brisk trot for his farm, which lay eight miles away on the hillside. On the way, we talked of various matters, mostly of farms and farming.

" Now that place up there," said Reed, pointing far up the hillside on our right to a noble old red-brick house encaved in elms, " is the finest farm hereabouts, and Tom Brock was the finest farmer, too, here or anywhere. His widow runs it now, and, for a woman, I must say she runs it pretty well."

" And has Brock been dead long ? " I asked. I liked to draw upon Reed's rich fund of talk

—talk consisting largely of local history, ancient and modern, repeatable and unrepeatable—so that I made a point, whenever possible, of dropping a provocative question.

"Yes," began Reed, "he died—let's see—ten years ago. A great, fine, upstanding man he was : as good a fellow all round as you could wish to meet ; and, Lord, how he could put away the drink when he'd a mind to ! Not that drink ever got the better of him. Nothing, dead or alive, ever got the better of Tom Brock. Still, he had his days, just once in a way like. I remember—Oh, it must be twelve years ago—I met him in town. It was market-day. I'd driven in in my buggy, as I always did, and put it up at the Angel. Tom used to put up somewhere else : I don't remember where. Anyhow, we met near the market towards evening. He'd had a good day, and I'd had a thundering good day too—I'd near on twenty-five pounds in my pocket in notes—and, besides, it was Tom's birthday. 'Look here, George,' he says to me. 'We'll go to the Rose and Crown and make an evening of it. The moon's full and a late drive home 'll do neither of us any harm.' So we went to the Rose and ordered supper. Well, Tom would have it that it was to be champagne. 'Beer for me,' he says, 'for everyday drinking, but a drop of champagne once in a way does you good.' So champagne it was.

"Well, what with the champagne and the grub, we soon got very hearty. Lord, it was wonderful fine talk that we talked that night, and it was finer still when we began putting down a bottle of old port after the champagne. Ah, wonderful talk ! I wish I could give you even a half of it now : but next morning— would you believe it ?—not a word of it could I remember. All I did remember was Tom's great shaking laugh and his jolly red face there across the table with the two eyes in it like little bits of blue glass.

"Well, we had a double whisky for luck, and then we began to think about getting home. It took a bit, of course, to get started. Not that we were drunk, mind you, but . . . well, you felt glad to take hold of a chair-back here and there, if you understand me, and it was a matter of going careful through the doorways. When we got out into the street, I turned to Tom and I says to him : 'Tom, where the devil did I put my buggy ?' And he says to me : 'Damned if I know, George. Where the

275

hell did I put my trap ? ' " Farmer Reed slapped his thigh and gave a roar. " However," he added, " I got home all right in the end : and so did Tom, so he told me next time we met. Yes, poor Tom Brock. It's ten years since he went : and a fine funeral he had ! His missus saw to that. Trust her to do things proper. Eh ! the tales that there are about that funeral. I saw something of it meself. I was there. I was farming in the Marsh at that time, and I and my missus came up in that little rattling train that starts from Felsing, down in the Marsh, with the others who came from those parts. There was Farmer Dixon and his missus who lived right out at Coles Hatch : a little, wiry fellow, he is, with a face like a shrivelled apple ; very different to Mrs. D. She was a great big woman like a prize sow, with the kind of eye that made people keep their distance. Then there was Miss Plimp, very thin and genteel, the retired schoolmistress from Felsing, and Jobson who kept The Anchor at Crome and Mrs. Jobson. He was a retired sergeant-major—a large, square, responsible sort of chap, very good company so long as he kept off the Boer War. She was a quick, neat little thing, a very taking little

party. The other two were old Widow Slapstone from Doomschurch way—a jolly round-
about old body she was, with round face and
round spectacles and a great chuckling laugh
as though a hen had got fixed up inside her
bodice ;—her, and a long, sour-faced, hay-rake
of a fellow called John Bouch, the Doomschurch sexton, who tried to speak like the parson. He was a bachelor and a teetotaller.
And then, of course, there was my missus and
meself.

"We all foregathered on the platform at
Felsing station and the nine of us came along
in the same compartment. Very grave and
proper we were in our best black, as fitted the
occasion. At first we all felt a bit awkward,
but you can't stay dignified long in a train that
joggles about, first to one side, then to the
other, fit to knock the dignity out of a
duke. So when the train got moving we
began to talk—at least the men did—mostly
about Tom Brock and the farm and what was
likely to happen to it. But the ladies kept
quiet. They were taking stock of each other's
clothes, I reckon, and each thinking her own
were the best. At least my missus was : she
told me as much afterwards.

"Well, when we arrived at Dore Station there was a wagonette waiting for us. Trust Mrs. Brock to do things in style. Of course, we had to sit pretty intimate, as you can imagine —nine in a wagonette. It was a case of ham to ham, I assure you ; and I found myself wedged up against Miss Plimp. 'A bit unusual, this, Miss Plimp,' I says to her. 'It is,' she says, and she looked away, a bit flustered like.

"Well, the funeral was like most funerals, only a bit grander : trust Mrs. Brock for that ! I don't remember much about it ; except that there was a great crowd of people there ; but there are one or two things I *do* remember. I remember the job they had to lift the coffin out of the hearse into the church, and out of the church again to the grave. He was a heavy man, was Tom, and the coffin was solid oak into the bargain ; and when they were trying to get it up, it suddenly came into my head— as these things will, you know—that what they wanted was Tom himself there to manage them, and I imagined his great hearty voice holloing at them : 'Now, steady there ! Ease 'er on the left, there. Now, all together when I say *lift*.' He'd have had the thing done in half the time. And I remember the moment, too, when they lowered him into his grave ; for it came over me suddenly then that Tom was gone for good, and that I'd lost a good friend. In fact he was a loss to the whole country, was Tom Brock. You don't see the like of him nowadays.

"When we got back to the farm it was well past the usual dinner time and we were all, as you can imagine, pretty peckish, so that it was all we could do to keep quiet when we went into the dining-room and saw the grub laid out there. God bless my soul ! You never saw such a spread. There was hams and standing pies, cheese, cakes, any amount of the best draught ale, and at least a dozen bottles of sherry wine. Yes, she buried him properly, and no mistake, did Mrs. Brock ! Tom himself would have been proud of that spread. We sat down twenty to table and Mrs. B. herself took the head. She was a fine figure of a woman—in fact, she still is—and she made a fine appearance that day in her new widow's-weeds : no expense spared, you may be certain, and a handkerchief with a black edge to it and all that. As soon as we had all settled down, she left us to it, and her brother, Jock Wilbraham, took the head.

"Well, you know, nobody can stand out for long against good food and good drink, and we all began to unbend a bit. Besides, as we all knew, Tom himself was a hearty eater and drinker and there was nothing he liked better than to see people enjoying themselves ; so we felt we owed it to him, in a manner of speaking, to do justice to the victuals. Everybody took beer except Bouch, the teetotal fellow from Doomschurch. He refused it. 'What ? No beer ?' says Jock Wilbraham. 'Then you'll take some stout, or maybe there's a drop of whisky in the house.' But when Bouch said he'd take water, Jock put his foot down. 'No, no,' he says, 'we can't have that. It shall never be said that a man drank water at Tom Brock's funeral. Come, Mr. Bouch, fill up your glass ' ; and Bouch filled it up, and I'm inclined to think that he was glad of the excuse. And no wonder, with even Miss Plimp, opposite him, taking her glass with the rest. After that he was all right ; in fact, when the sherry went round he took his whack at that too. But Miss Plimp jibbed at the sherry, just at first. 'Come along now, Miss Plimp,' said Dixon, who was sitting next her ; 'surely you're not going to give in, A drop of good sherry never did anyone any harm,' and he filled her up a good glassful. She took to it very kindly, I'm bound to say, and, what's more, she remarked that it was uncommon good.

"Well, after a bit, Jobson took out his watch. When you're proprietor of a public-house, you see, you get used to keeping a sharp eye on the time. 'Bless me !' he says, 'it's five o'clock already and it's six miles good to the station. We Marsh folk will have to be trotting if we want to catch the train.'

"'You sit tight,' shouts Jock Wilbraham. 'The wagonette's going to take you to the station, so you've a good half-hour yet.' So we all had another drink and got talking again till the wheels on the gravel brought us to our senses.

"Well, we packed ourselves into the wagonette as well as we could, and I assure you it was a much more difficult matter than when we arrived : and when the driver touched the horses we all gave a lurch—all of a piece like —that almost tipped the two at the edge out of the trap. 'Well, well !' said Dixon, with a deep sigh. 'All good things must come to an end. I'm only sorry that poor Tom Brock

himself wasn't there to enjoy the occasion.'
After that, nobody said much on the way to the
station. We were all sort of getting our bear-
ings, I reckon—finding out what we *could* do
and what we *couldn't*. Old Mother Dixon was
opposite me. Her face was as red as a beet
and shining like a glazed mug, but her expression was desperate serious. Jobson looked
mighty serious too, till he caught my eye
and gave me a look that nearly did for us
both. Miss Plimp, however, wasn't serious at
all : she had on a smile that just stayed there.
She didn't seem to know about it, but there
it was. Bouch was at the end—the dangerous
end : he was taken up with holding on his
hat and trying to stop himself dropping off
into the road. The rest, of course, were on my
side.

" We pulled ourselves together for the station,
and got into the train very decently. It was
when the train started that the trouble began.
It was a joggly little train, as I've told you, and
when it began dancing us up and down like a
carriage-load of babies . . . well, we all began
to laugh, somehow. Then it took the corner
towards Beckland before we were quite ready
for it, and we all swung out to the west, and

little Mrs. Jobson and Bouch who had the window-seats on the outside of the curve got the whole weight of us. Miss Plimp, on the inside, was flattened up tight against Jobson like a fly on a flypaper. Force is force, and, struggle as she would, she couldn't get away from him till she dropped off him when the train had got into the straight again. After that comes the long straight bit where the train always begins to do a gallop. It gallops on the right as far as Broxop and then it switches over and gallops on the left till it comes to Windover corner where it slings you over west again and then runs smooth for a while to prepare you for the last almighty shake-up as it rattles you into Felsing.

" The train was late that evening and it was putting on speed. In the Broxop stretch old Mother Slapstone lost her spectacles. She had been sitting there more peaceable than other folk. Weight tells on these occasions, so being heavier than most, she sat steadier. But suddenly the train gave an extra bump and her spectacles just dropped off her nose. She made a dive for them, but unfortunately little Dixon made a dive for them at the same time, and they both upset each other, I suppose. Anyway, down they both went on to the floor. They were so mixed up at first that we couldn't get them sorted, and old Mother Slapstone started her laughing and cackling. It was that, I fancy, which set us off—all, that is, except Mrs. Dixon. She sat square all the time as sour as milk in a thunderstorm. Well, we laughed on the right as far as Broxop, and we laughed on the left till Windover, and then Windover curve tumbled us all over into the corner and shook us up together like a dish of peas. 'Lord, Lord!' said Dixon, as we were straightening ourselves up for Felsing, 'how Tom Brock would have laughed at this!'

"At Felsing station we helped one another out. Miss Plimp couldn't seem to get the hang of it, so Jobson just whipped her up and set her down on the platform like a kid. It was late autumn, and it had been coming up thick all afternoon, so that by the time we got to the cross-roads beyond the station it was almost pitch dark. We separated there. The Jobsons and the Dixons took the road to the right for Crome and Coles Hatch, I and my missus kept straight on, and the rest went off to the left to Felsing village and Doomschurch.

"Well, I only picked up bit by bit what happened to every one after that. Little Mrs. Jobson told me herself what came of *them*. 'You see, it's an awkward road on a dark night, with all them forks and turnings,' she said to me. 'Now out with it, Mrs. J.,' says I : 'don't you begin trying to excuse it.' 'Well, we never doubted that we were getting along very nicely, Fred and me,' she says, 'till we got to the very door. Then Fred couldn't get the key to fit. He tried and tried, but it was no good, so he struck a match, and then I caught sight of the sign. "Goodness gracious me !" I says. "Look at that, Fred ! It isn't The Anchor at all : it's The Black Bull." "The Black Bull ?" says Fred. "Then we're at Chubdyke." And sure enough, would you believe me, we'd got to the wrong village.' 'I would, Mrs. J.,' says I, 'seeing the state you was in.'

"Well, the Dixons came off worse than that. I got their story from Snaith the ditcher, who happened to be going home late. He followed them up on the road. The old woman had cut up rough about something, seemingly, and they were having a bit of a row. The road runs along the edge of a dyke thereabouts, and the

285

next thing Snaith heard was a great splash. The old woman had gone in, head over ears. Well, of course, it was like trying to rescue a prize pig. Dixon alone wasn't much good, or perhaps he left her to soak a bit on purpose, for there's nothing like cold water on these occasions. Anyhow, he and Snaith together got her landed at last. That's what comes of cutting up rough on a dark night. I heard afterwards that before they got home she made Dixon wet himself all over and they told the girl who dried their things that it had been a soaking wet night, which was true enough as far as they were concerned.

"As for the rest, Mother Slapstone was all right. 'Thank Providence,' she said, when she wished us good-night at the cross-roads, 'Thank Providence, my dears, I've Jim and the cart waiting for me at Felsing.' About the teetotal fellow and Miss Plimp, the story goes that she . . . well, she simply collared him. I can't vouch for the truth of it, mind ; but I know for certain that he didn't get home to Doomschurch till nine o'clock next morning, and, what's more, they made a match of it and were married a couple of months later. Which shows what drink may let you in for."

"And what about yourself and Mrs. Reed?"
I asked.

"Ha, ha!" roared Farmer Reed. "If you
want that story you must ask one of the others."